# Bouquet of Daisies

## Nicholette Kay

# Contents

# Dedication

To Adam, for supporting me and encouraging me to publish this book. I love you.

# Trigger Warning

This book contains mentions of sexual assault and rape, though you will not read about it happening to a character, it is mentioned.

# Bouquet of Daisies

# Prologue

The golden rays of the sun illuminated around his face. Those piercing blue eyes smiling back at me, I lean in to kiss him. As we pull away, I can't help but smile. "Blake, I can't wait until the day I become your wife." I pushed back his jet-black hair as he chuckled and moved his face to my hand, kissing it and taking it into his.

His thumb runs over my newest accessory, "Mrs. Elizabeth Taylor does have a nice ring to it." I nestle my head on his shoulder. This picnic was perfect, this day was perfect, my life was perfect.

# Chapter One

## Three Years Later

*Elizabeth*

My eyelids feel like they have bricks attached to them. I finally force them open and I reach for the glass of Merlot on the coffee table. I dozed off watching *Cupcake Wars* yet again. I down the drink in my hand as I stand and walk into the kitchen. "That stupid dream." I sigh and search for a bottle to refill the glass. I hear the buzzing of my phone: four texts and two missed calls from Katie, my sister.

3:34 pm

Bethy!

It's 4:15. I close the wine cabinet and settle on a glass of sweet tea. I'm excited to see Katie, she's ten years younger than me, so anytime we can see each other it is extremely rare. She turned sixteen last month and finally got her license, and now she's constantly looking for an excuse to drive.

The door slams open, "Bethy!"

I smile and look around the corner, "Hey Katie cat, sorry I was taking a nap earlier." She engulfs me in a hug, and I have to catch myself or we would fall over. I have never understood how someone so petite could have so much strength. I'm also just as small, but I can hardly open a jar of pickles without help.

"It's okay, I was just worried about you. I know the cake shop is really starting to take off now, we just haven't heard from you in a little while."

I kiss her forehead and push her hair back. "I'm sorry, I'm sure mom and dad are worried sick about me. I promise to stop by this weekend. Who knew owning a cake shop could be so time consuming?"

I know school starting last month has stressed Katie out, and I should be checking in on her more. She gives a shrug and turns to make her way to the fridge. She stumbles over air, it's a wonder how that girl has never broken a bone, she catches herself on the counter.

Her hit caused something to fall on the top shelf; Katie reached up to fix what she knocked over. Seeing the frame alone sent my stomach into a spiral and I felt heat creeping into my cheeks. I don't need to look to see the picture of Blake and I on Christmas Eve six years ago. We were cuddled up together; the love evident in our blue eyes. It was our first Christmas together.

Katie's sorry eyes look up at me as I take the picture and return it to the shelf. After a moment of silence, Katie takes a deep breath. "Do you miss him?" I nod, Blake is never a topic anyone dared to bring up to me, his name alone caused my heart to rip.

"It's been two years since your wedding was called off! Will you please tell me what happened? What did he do?" She pleads.

"No!" I snap, and Katie winces. I instantly regret it, I almost never raise my voice at my little sister. I clench and unclench my fists, trying to regain my composure. I take a deep breath and look at my sister. "I'm sorry- It's just not something I want to discuss. Bl-Blake." I force his name out. "He is off the table."

She's quiet, her eyes staring back at me before she releases a breath. "Well, what about trying to date again? You are like the most beautiful girl in town, and I *know* all the single guys would love to have the chance to take you out. If you don't start dating again, I'm going to sign you up for the next season of *The Bachelor*."

I shake my head as I get a pot out to boil water. "Yeah, please don't do that. Seriously, I have no time to date, not with me just opening my cake shop."

"I just think- never mind." She huffs, "And everyone says teenagers are stubborn." She mumbles. I chuckle to myself.

She takes the sausage out of the fridge and hands it to me. "Please, please tell me you're making gumbo again." And just like that the dating conversation is dropped, thank goodness. I'm too tired to get into that argument again.

Katie turns her Spotify on and dances around the kitchen while singing into a whisk. I continue working on the food, singing along with my sister. She jumps onto the couch and pretends as if she is performing for a crowd.

My sister is the care-free one of the two of us, she can make a show of herself no matter where we are. I am always prim and proper. Katie swirls around me and unclips my pin straight hair and watches it cascade over my shoulders. "Have you ever thought about getting highlights? Or going blonde?"

I laugh and shake my head. "No, what? Are you thinking about going blonde?" I raise an eyebrow her way.

She shrugs and plops onto the couch. "Dad says I will look like mom if I go blonde. I was thinking about trying it out."

I place the cover on the pot and follow her into the living room. "I agree, if you do it, I have to be the first to see it." That wins me an excited nod, Katie curls into me and turns on a baking show for me. We sit and watch for a few minutes when there is a knock on my door. I glance down at her, raising an eyebrow at her, and she gives a shrug.

I curiously opened the door, "Hello?" I say to the unfamiliar guy in front of me. He must be no older than me, he has a 5 o'clock shadow on his face and his ashy blonde hair is messed up. His wrinkled-up t-shirt tells me that he has had quite a day.

He steps back the moment our eyes meet. "Oh, sorry ma'am, I have the wrong house." His fingers clumsily fumble with a piece of paper as he backs down the four steps to the sidewalk.

"Who are you looking for?" I ask.

He looks shyly up at me, red hinting at his cheeks. "Um, Gavin Johnson. I'm staying with him for a while until I find a place to live."

I look down at the bags resting by his feet. "Oh! You must be Patrick; Gavin was telling me about his friend that is moving to town." I smile at him and stick my hand out. "I'm Elizabeth." He grabs my hand and lightly squeezes it, a small smile spreading on his lips.

I point down the street. "He lives just three houses down. But I'm sure you have had quite a day from your travels. My sister and I are cooking supper, and it should be ready soon if you would like to join."

As if on cue, Katie appears in the doorway and sticks her hand out. "Eat with us! Bethy loves to have people over." She turns and winks at me, grabbing his hand, she drags him into the house.

"Well, it doesn't seem like you have an option now." I laugh and grab his bags and sit them by my front door before heading back to the kitchen. "Patrick? Would you like a glass of sweet tea?"

"He would love one!" Katie shouts. I roll my eyes; I fill a glass and turn around to see my wide-eyed sister standing right behind me.

"He's *sooo* cute!" She grins. "You should ask him out, sissy. I bet he would say yes. He blushes every time you say something or look at him."

"Oh hush. We just met."

"Watch. Bring him his tea." She earns herself another eye roll, and I follow her into the living room.

"So, Patrick, where did you move here from?"

"I'm from Dallas, Gavin and I started a contracting business together. But I actually was raised in Nolensville, so it's nice to be back to my roots."

I smile back at him. "Oh, how funny! I grew up here as well. Not many people from Nolensville, or even Nashville make their way back!" I look down at his hands, they are not too callused.

"So, you're a handyman?" I raise an eyebrow.

He chuckles and yes, his cheeks turn that soft hue again. "Sorta. I can do fixer-uppers and small projects; the big stuff is all for Gav. I'm more of the brains of the duo." He glances over at my phone that just vibrated.



I flip my phone upside down and look back at Patrick. "What do you mean brains?"

"Well, I do all the communication and visionary work. I can go into a room and tell you exactly what could be done to improve the space. Gavin takes my ideas and makes them reality."

"That's awesome! Maybe you can help me with some stuff around my house. I just moved in last year and have been dying to make the place cozier. It's a little too builder-grade for me."

"I would love to help you." He smiles at me, I can't help but notice that he has a kind smile. There is a bit of an uncomfortable pause, maybe because Katie is staring us down, or maybe because I haven't had a guy over since Blake. To avoid the silence and thinking about that one topic, I get up and check on the food, thankfully it's all done. I scoop the food into three separate bowls and set them on the counter. "Everything is ready!"

I sense Patrick behind me and turn to hand him a bowl, "Is that gumbo?" He takes a deep inhale and breathes out with a grin on his face. "Smells just like New Orleans."

I can't help but smile at him. "Well, that's because our mom was born and raised there. She taught me everything I know about southern cuisine! Remind me to make you some beignets at some point."

"I will definitely take you up on that offer." He takes his bowl from me and heads to the living room. Katie grabs her own bowl and bumps me with her hip.

She covers her mouth, "You know, I have a good feeling about this guy. Ask him out."

I furrow my brows at her. "He is just being friendly. And I told you, I'm not dating, end of story." I turn around and head to the couch to sit next to my guest. I notice he has already eaten a good portion of his gumbo, and some of the sauce is on his cheek. I giggle and hand him a napkin off the side table, I point to my cheek to show him where he needs to wipe. His face quickly turns red as he wipes the sauce off.

"Thanks, ma'am. This is delicious, by the way."

Katie leans over the back of the couch, her face in between both of us. "If you like her cooking, just wait till you try her baking." She rounded back around the couch and plops down in my armchair and happily began eating.

"Well, it seems like you know your way around the kitchen." Patrick turns to face me.

"Well, yes. I own my own cake shop. But I can make all sorts of stuff, my dad taught me all about cooking and baking when I was a girl. So, if you want it, I can make it."

"You should stop by her shop tomorrow to try something. It will make you fall in love." Katie pipes in before taking a mouthful of gumbo.

A hold a spoon up to my mouth, "Well, I can't promise you'll fall in love, but I certainly would love to see you stop by."

"In that case, I'm sure I can make time to stop by tomorrow. What's the name of your store?"

"The Flour Shop." I smile, as he laughs at my pun.

"That's amazing, what made you want to open your own place."

"Well, as I said, my dad taught me to bake and I have always loved it. I started cooking for fun in high school, helping dad and sometimes taking charge of dinner. I started selling cake pops and creating my own flavors, and next thing I know I'm making hundreds each week for birthday parties.

So, I started taking decorating classes for cakes to have more of a clientele. Now I have enough business that I have my own store, with a perfect sized kitchen." I smile at him, and he grins back at me.

"Well, I can't wait to try it."

The three of us sit and finish our food, Katie states she has homework and makes her way out with a flash but not without winking at me. It's only 7:45 now, that girl always finishes her schoolwork during class or study hall, and with her insistence on my dating life, she definitely is trying to set this thing up.

After I hug her bye, I grab the dishes and go to the kitchen to start cleaning up. Patrick starts drying as I wash the bowls. "You don't have to do this, you're my guest." I smile at him.

"But I want to, you made dinner and offered me some, it's the least I can do for your hospitality." I glance at him, and I see the soft pink fading from his cheeks. Maybe Katie is onto something, or maybe she is being her overly optimistic self. Once we finish the dishes, I grab a glass of wine and offer one to him which he politely declines. We head back to the couch, and I grab a blanket, I position myself on the couch to settle in.

Something about this guy makes me feel like I have known him for years. I give him the remote, "We have watched enough baking, you can pick out a movie, unless you want to get over to Gavin's."

He takes a second to answer me. "No, I can stay for a while, I had such a long flight from Texas. My plane was delayed for three hours. Relaxing here with you is so much better than walking into instant work plans with Gav."

He scrolls through the selections. After a few minutes of scrolling, he settles on *The Truman Show* and grabs another blanket off the back of the couch and pulls it over his legs.

"So," he starts, his eyes still focused on the tv, "Are you from New Orleans?"

"Nope, born and raised in Tennessee! I've actually lived here in Nolensville my whole life.

He quickly turns to face me. "No way, so did I!" He is clearly thinking for a second, his eyes are searching my face for something, I just don't know what. "Wait, Elizabeth, did you have a neighbor you played with as a kid? I remember playing with a girl named Elizabeth growing up."

I laugh and shake my head. "I don't remember anyone named Patrick. But also, that was almost 20 years ago."

"Well, it was worth a shot. That would be a crazy coincidence." He smiles back at me.

"It definitely would be. I was always playing with my golden retriever and a few of the neighborhood kids."

Patrick's brow furrows, and he stares at me for a second clearly trying to recall something once more. "My neighbor also had a golden retriever. It made me always want to have a dog of my own." He starts laughing, "Its name was Maple, I only remember because I tried feeding her pancakes once and her dad got so mad at me."

My heart leaps at the name of the dog, I quickly turn to him and grab his arm, "Wait! My dog was named Maple, and I had a friend always feeding her whatever his mom cooked! Wow! I'm going to have to ask my mom about you."

I stare at him for a minute, searching his eyes, his face, for any type of memory of him. But nothing would come. "You would think I could recognize you." I stare at him a second longer and he gazes back at me. My throat suddenly goes dry, so I quickly turn away and take a sip of my wine.

I can't help it, but my mind goes to Blake and everything that happened. Suddenly I feel like I need to rush Patrick out of here. What if he does get any ideas like Katie suggested? No, I can keep that away, he doesn't seem to be flirting with me. Plus, we just met so he doesn't know enough about me to even have any kind of feelings. But I feel like we are already old friends. I force myself from the spiral I am going on, and I take a breath, "So Texas?"

He nods back at me. "Yep, I moved to Texas and stayed there until I moved back to go to the University of Tennessee to get a degree in accounting. I went on a big group spring break trip to Cancun during my junior year, and that's where I really got to know Gavin. I tagged along with him in some construction gigs which is where I learned about my, I guess, reconstruction talent.

I moved back to Texas to work in finance until Gavin called me up one day to start our own company. I have just worked on the office side of the company, but that has been getting hard to do remotely. So here I am."

"So, are you going to be out there building things with him?" I wonder.

"Gav wants me to. My dad taught me the basics when I was a kid, so I'll be assisting with some projects until I get a hold of the ropes. We have hired some workers for us, but now that I'm here, we can really get the ball moving. I'm getting all the logistics finished up this week and then it should be smooth sailing."

"Well, I'm glad you're here"

"Thanks." He says with a yawn. "Well, sorry we missed most of the movie, but I need to get settled in and I'm sure Gavin is freaking out."

"Yes, and you had quite a long day of traveling, I'm sorry to have kept you."

"Don't worry about it, it was nice to make a friend on my first day."

I smile and get up to grab his bags. "It was nice meeting you, again, so, I'll see you around?"

"Most definitely." He takes the bags from me and hesitates for a second before turning around. "Thanks for the dinner and company."

A wide grin spread across my face. "Anytime, Patrick."

I shut the door and stare at it for a moment and realize I'm smiling. I actually feel happy and tonight started so dreary. I think Patrick's smile came to mind but suddenly his image got intertwined with Blake's. My stomach lurches thinking of him, and I have to hold back a sob. I pour myself one more glass of wine to help soothe myself. As I taste the sweet red, images flash through my head quickly reminding me about how I don't deserve happiness anymore. I continue gulping down my beverage until I finally feel calm. Hopefully I can go to bed tonight without any nightmares.

# Chapter Two

## PATRICK

I stumble towards Gavin's house in a daze. Did tonight really happen? Elizabeth felt like she'd been pulled from my dreams and set down in front of me. Well, I guess all those fairytales are real, there is such a thing as love at first sight. By the time I knock on the door, guilt pulls on me, I'm three hours late. The door swings open, and I'm greeted by Gavin's raised brows and rumpled sweatpants tell me- he's been waiting to go to bed.

"Where have you been? You were supposed to be here hours ago." He demands.

Heat crept into my cheeks. Before I could speak, realization lit Gavin's face.

"You met a girl. Dude, you haven't been here for six hours, and you met a girl! Who is it?"

I shake my head, half in awe at how easily he can read me. Then again, we've been friends for 6 years. "Her name is Elizabeth."

A knowing grin spreads across Gavin's face, he crosses his arms. "Elizabeth Riley. I should have guessed. She's exactly your type: sweet, perfect, annnnd unavailable."

My heart plummets.

"She's not taken," he adds quickly, sparking an ounce of hope, "just... she doesn't date. Hasn't since her engagement ended two years ago."

Relief and doubt start to battle within me. What chance do I really have with someone who refuses to date? I have practically no experience, not like Gavin; he thrived on socializing while I've never been into hookups. I have only dated a few girls through college, but since graduation five years ago I have just focused on work.

I sigh. "Well... maybe that can change? We had a good time tonight. She acted like she'd want to see me again."

Gavin raises a brow. "I hate to burst your bubble dude, but she's a people person. She loves getting to know people, and people love her. I'm just looking out for you, bro."

Stacey, Gavin's wife, appears behind him. I'm assuming we woke her up as her hair was going in every direction. "Hi, Pat. Are y'all going to bed anytime soon?"

Gavin puts his arm around her waist and kisses her forehead, a pang of jealousy hits. Why have I spent all this time not looking for someone? "Yeah, just a few minutes. Go back to bed, hun." She pads back towards their bedroom, and I make my way into their living room with my bags.

"Gav, before you head up, what happened with the engagement?"

He shrugs. "No one knows. They were crazy in love, then one day the ring was gone and so was he. Moved to another state. Nobody's seen him since. Elizabeth doesn't talk about it."

I nod and walk towards the guest room. "Gotcha. Well...see you tomorrow. I won't keep you up any longer."

In the guest room, I undress and get into bed. I stare at the ceiling but all I can see is Elizabeth's blue eyes. Her smile is now ingrained in my mind. Even if she doesn't want to date me, I need her in my life.

The next morning, I wake up and grab a bowl of cereal. Gav and Stacey are already gone; probably to work, errands, or whatever married people do. Guilt pokes at me again for keeping them up late, but I shake it off and unpack. It doesn't even take me five minutes, living out of a suitcase for a month would be rough, but hopefully, I'd find a place soon. Otherwise, I will see a lot of laundry days in my future.

After taking a much-needed shower and shaving, I decide to go out and see the town. It's been about a year since I was last in Nolensville, and that was only for a short weekend to help with a project.  Once I put on a brown button up, I head out the door. I decided to go to Historic Nolensville; there are apparently several coffee shops that have popped up since the last time I was here that I would love to try.

Historic Nolensville is just a handful of shops on both sides of the road. I grab a coffee and sit outside, watching traffic. Childhood memories come flooding back to me, my mom used to take me shopping here. Every spring they hold a festival where I would run between different treat booths, begging my mom for more sweets. I smile at the memory and take another sip of coffee.

I scan the storefronts, but most were women's boutiques. I guess I'll have to make a trip to Cool Springs Mall for clothes.

Then I see it: The Flour Shop. My heart leaps knowing Elizabeth is just a few steps away. Without hesitation, I stand and quickly cross the street.

The smell of vanilla wraps around me as a bell chimes overhead.

"Hello!" Her voice sounds like a melody. I glance around the bakery; there is a case full of colorful treats and different shades of brown pastries. The soft greens of the shop makes me feel at home. A bouquet of flowers sits on top of the case, and matching flowers dot each table. I smile, loving her use of a double entendre.

Elizabeth appears out of the back room, she's wearing a pink apron over a white t-shirt. A smudge of flour marks her cheek, but boy does she look stunning. "Patrick! I didn't know if I would be seeing you today." She walks over and gives me a gentle hug. Her hair smells like coconuts and frosting.

I laugh and point at her cheek. "You got something there."

She quickly wipes it off with her sleeve. "Oh- thanks, so what brought you here?"

"I was just grabbing coffee and spotted your place. So, I thought I'd say hello. Plus, I told you I'd come by."

Her eyes sparkle, and warmth rushes to my face. I look away quickly to try to hide my blush.

"Well, I'm glad you did. Would you like to try something? Cake, cake pops, cupcakes, cookies?"

"Surprise me."

She grins and disappears into the back. When she returns, she holds out a plate.

I raise a brow. "That's pie. That wasn't on the list."

She giggles and shrugs. "I've been perfecting my pies, and you seem like an honest guy." Before I could react, she slid the fork into my mouth. Apple pie, just like my grandma's. Sweet, crisp apples, the perfect amount of cinnamon. I grin. "I would eat the whole thing if you let me. This is incredible."

"Really?" Her face lights up.

"Really."

Elizabeth jumps up and hugs me. I laugh and I don't hesitate to wrap my arms around her. My heart pounds as I wrap my arms around her.

"Thanks, Patrick." She spins away and returns with the whole pie. "So, not too much cinnamon?"

"Nope. Just like Grandma used to make."

She nods contently with my answer and starts taking pictures of the pie. I lean against the counter and watch her. "So, is this a bakery since you have an assortment?"

She answers with a small shrug. "Sort of. I mainly like to focus on cakes and decorating them. Or decorating cookies, I love decorating and being creative with desserts.

Since most people don't eat cake except for special occasions, I have a small assortment for anyone who craves something sweet. Besides, I focus a lot on cake pops since that is really what got me started."

"Well, that makes sense, the smell coming from your shop would bring me in."

"Thank you, Patrick. So, what are you up to today?" Her head tilts to the side as she waits for my answer.

"I'm shopping for some clothes, and things to get by. I'm hoping to check out some places to stay as well. I would like to be out of Gav's by the end of the month. Stacey is a patient person...but not *that* patient." I chuckle and sit at one of her round tables. She follows and sits by me, propping her chin on her palm.

"What an adventurous day for you." She laughs. "Do you want to grab dinner later? I can help you narrow down some places if you want. Nolensville has changed a lot since we were kids, and it can be hard to find a nice place."

I can't help the smile that spreads across my face. "I would love that, what would you like?"

"Pizza," she answers instantly. "If that's okay. I just want a low-key night at home."

"Pizza it is." I finish off my coffee that I have been nursing all morning. I stand to throw it away and hover next to the door, "I'll see you later then?"

"Yes, my place at 6?"

"Perfect."

━ℓℓ━

Shopping filled the afternoon, I couldn't get much without a place of my own. I ended up going to Birchwood Market to just get some nice t-shirts, button downs, and some more jeans. I donated most of my clothes in Texas so that I wouldn't have to pay a ton on moving. Shipping my car here had cost a fortune, and I had just enough to scrape by for now.

As for rentals, nothing stood out. Maybe it's because of my job in remodeling, but there was an issue with every place I went into. Plus, the further out of Nolensville I got, the more

I thought about how Elizabeth would be further than a few steps.

Eventually I gave up and headed back to the house, where I am sitting on the couch now, trying to not constantly check my phone as I count down the hours to see that beautiful brunette.

I set an alarm for five to get ready so that I could be ready and not be late. I hear the alarm going off on my phone in my room and my pulse quickens. I look into the mirror, and I rake my hand through my hair, and spritz myself in cologne, but Gavin's warning is still echoing in my head.

At six sharp, I walk over to Elizabeth's, proud of myself for not running late like always. She opens the door before I can knock. My hand hangs in the air and I bring it to my side as I study her. Her hair is tied in a messy bun, leggings, and an oversized t-shirt replacing her work outfit. Somehow, she grows more stunning every time I see her.

She hugs me and hands me water before she goes into the kitchen and pours herself wine.

"Did you have any big cake orders today?"

She shakes her head. "Not today. But my mom is a wedding planner, and she is pitching me to one of her new clients. So, fingers crossed."

She holds up both of her hands with her fingers crossed, then reaches for her phone and starts scrolling on it. "Pepperoni and green peppers?"

"Only the best two toppings on a pizza," I nod back to her, "How'd you know?"

She grins over at me "Well, you just seem like a guy with good taste."

We sink onto her cream couch, and she begins telling me stories about her creations, showing me pictures of them as she tells me exactly who each of them were for. She also shows me cakes she would like to make, flavor experiments, and even pies.

A knock sounds at her door, and I grab the pizza and pay for it. I settle in next to her on the couch. We eat in comfortable silence, and I can't help but think about how I could get used to this.

"I needed that" She sighs. "Sometimes I forget to eat while I'm working. Funny, right? Working with food all day and starving myself." I laugh and take our plates and put them in her sink.

"Would you like to go on a walk with me?" She asks.

"Yeah, sure!" I head to the entrance and hold the door open for her. I motion outside, "Lead the way."

We stroll side by side, our path lit up by the orange glow of streetlights. I keep sneaking glances at any chance I am able, though she didn't seem to notice, or maybe she didn't care. We keep having friendly conversations, but nothing overly flirtatious. I guess she is uninterested, Gav was right.

"So," she starts, smirking, "I called my mom today to ask if she remembers you. *Apparently*, we were inseparable. We played together rain or shine, we even got married the day after my sixth birthday."

I can't help but laugh, "I don't remember *that*. I just remember the heartbreak when we moved to Texas."

She nudges me playfully with her elbow, "How dare you up and leave your broken-hearted wife like that."

My chest tightens at the word *wife*. I give her a mock bow. "My sincerest apologies, ma'am, how can I ever make it up to you?"

She taps her chin in playful thought. "Hmm.. How about a daisy?"

The memory hit me- I used to bring her one every time I visited. Spotting a wild daisy in the field, I plucked it and handed it to her. "For you, my dear. Must be one of the last of the season, lucky for me."

She spins it between her fingers, creating a blur of white. "In that case, I suppose I can forgive you now."

We make it back to her house, and she pours herself another glass of wine and offers me another bottle of water. As she is in the kitchen, I turn the TV on, it was on the *Food Network*, her life really does revolve around food.

"Is this where you go for inspiration?"

"Oh, sometimes. I grab a lot of cooking inspiration from here, since my passion is mostly baking. Katie loves to come over for dinner, so I like to use her as my guinea pig. When she was younger, she would act like she was a judge on *MasterChef* and rate everything I did." She chuckles.

Her gaze lingers on the TV, so I steal another glance at her. Tiredness has settled into her face, she looks exhausted though she didn't say it. I stood, deciding she needs to get some sleep and she is too nice to tell me to go.

She furrows her eyebrows in confusion when she sees me stand. "Where are you going?"

"I don't want to overstay my welcome, you can get some rest for work tomorrow."

She smiles softly. "Thank you."

She reaches for my phone, tapping her number in, and then texts herself. "There. Now you have no reason to not talk to me." My heart thuds, maybe I was wrong? This is a pretty bold way to give someone your number.

She smiles up at me. "Thanks for coming, I had fun." I hug her quickly before heading back to Gavin's.

Gavin and Stacey are watching a movie but pause it when I come into the living room. "Before you ask, I've been with Elizabeth today. We had dinner, went for a walk, and she gave me her number. I don't know, but I think there is something there. She even brought up that we are fake married." My heart leaps at the thought of marrying her. Something in me keeps nudging me, telling me she's the one.

Stacey sighs and shakes her head. "Patrick, she's sweet, but sometimes too sweet. She flirts without realizing it. You're new, she's welcoming. But she's turned down every guy since the breakup. I'm sorry, I know this isn't what you want to hear, but we don't want you to get hurt."

Gavin nods. "She's great, but don't blind yourself. You deserve someone amazing, don't miss out chasing someone who won't give you a chance." He claps his hand on my shoulder. "Now get some rest. We have a big client meeting tomorrow. Please, *please*, don't be late."

I chuckle, "I'll try."

I lay in bed that night, replaying the past two days in my head and thinking about Stacey's words. Since college, I have been so focused on my career that I haven't really thought about settling down. But since meeting Elizabeth, that's all I can think about. I want her in my life, however she'll let me.

# Chapter Three



*Elizabeth*

The past 2 weeks have been a blur. Since my mom is a wedding planner, she recommended a bride named Tiffany to me for her wedding cake. I drew out cake sketches, created their samples, and secured them in the books. Tiffany was so excited about the cake that she told all her friends about me. This led to a flood of bookings for this weekend alone: cookies and for a baby shower, cupcakes for a birthday party, and three pies for an upcoming cookout. On top of that, I also added muffins and scones to my daily menu to draw in more customers.

After a busy day working on these events, I finally have a moment and my employee, Caroline, is covering the counter for foot traffic. I take a seat, sighing at the instant relief my feet feel. I slide my phone out of my apron pocket, and I can't help but smile when I see Patrick's name among the notifications.



It's been about a week since the last time I saw Patrick. Although I have many friends in town, getting to know someone new is so refreshing. He's so easy-going and doesn't mind that I just want to watch tv after work.

My other friends mean well, but they still tiptoe around me after three years, always wanting answers that I'm not ready to give. I pretend Blake never existed. With Patrick, Blake truly doesn't exist, he doesn't know about my broken engagement or my broken heart. There's no pretending with him, I can just be me.

After a ten-minute break, I walk to the kitchen and get back into decorating the cake I have been working on for the past several hours.

When I got home, I immediately take a shower, now that I am finally clean and free of my flour residue I can focus on my dinner. I decide to make myself a fettuccine alfredo with a glass of Chardonnay. I turn on some music and sway as I make my pasta and take long sips of my wine. When the food is done cooking, I plate it and plop onto the couch and turn on *The Food Network*.

As I take the last bite when I hear a knock at my door. I hurry and put my bowl in the sink, then I run over and swing the door wide open. I can't help but grin up at Patrick.

"Hey there!" I wrap my arms around him for a quick hug.

"So, tell me about what has been keeping you busy." He says as he shoves his hands into his jean pockets, he's wearing a khaki t-shirt that is helping his green eyes shine.

I walk down the few steps and begin catching up with him on the past couple weeks as we begin our walk.

"I'm going to have to come in this weekend to finish up on the cookies and the cupcakes. See? I told you I don't have much of a life outside of The Flour Shop."

"Well, would you like any help? I can't bake to save my life, but I can wash dishes?" He shoots a crooked grin at me.

"Wow, that's so kind of you, but I can't ask you to do that."

"Well good thing you aren't asking, and I'm offering." He fully smiles at me, and I realize I can't argue with that.

"Okay, Friday night. Most of these orders go out on Saturday morning."

The sunset washes the streets in gold, the air is crisp with an early fall breeze. "What about you? How is work and the house search going?"

He gives a small shrug and sighs. "Work is fine, I have been doing it remotely so nothing much has changed except that I am here now, and I can now work directly with Gavin and go to the suppliers. The house search, well....it's okay. Nothing has seemed appealing to me, I'm not sure if it's because I work in the housing world."

"I don't want to live in the craziness of Nashville, and all the new places here in Nolensville are family homes. It's unfortunate there are so few townhomes available here, I love this neighborhood." He sighed and looked up at the house we were passing by. "I'm thinking about looking in Franklin, there are so many options there."

"Oh wow," I nod, "Well something will pop up soon. Franklin is nice and there is a lot to do there. I understand your hesitation, Nolensville is a great little town. I love how quiet it is."

I shiver as a cold breeze blows. "I'm so thankful that we get some chilly nights in September, it makes me so ready for fall, not this fake fall nonsense." I chuckle.

"Oh, I agree, this definitely beats the Texas heat. Even the days here aren't so bad, it was in the one hundreds there almost every day this summer. It's nice to step outside and not immediately start sweating." He laughs. "Well, let's get you back home so you don't catch a cold."

We turn around and head back to my house. Once inside, I grab my glass of wine and sit crisscrossed on the couch next to him. He pulls out his phone and shows me photos of kitchens and bathrooms his company has renovated. My favorite was a tiny galley kitchen they'd transformed into an open space with a bright island. I glance at my own cramped counters, imagining the possibilities.

I turn on reruns of *The Office* knowing he probably doesn't want to watch my never-ending stream of cooking shows. As we watch the episode, I try to suppress a yawn as I suddenly feel my body demanding rest. My head bobbed once, and then twice, before he notices and rises quietly. "I think someone needs to get to bed." A corner of his mouth lifts.

I walk him out, then go straight to my bedroom, falling into bed. I wake up in the middle of the night with my face damp, another nightmare. Here we go again.

❧ ☙

Friday comes and we are as busy as ever. I have had many customers coming in to work in the bakery throughout the day. They stop at one of the various coffee shops and come here for a pastry and settle in for work. I sent Caroline home around two. We are typically busiest in the mornings, and I just need help with customers as I was making all the sweets for this weekend.

At three I had a rush of people come in and camp out until I closed at five.

Now, I'm elbow-deep in frosting creating various colorings when I hear a knock at the door. I looked at the time, it's only been an hour since I closed so surely no one is trying to buy something. I look at my frosting covered hands and hurry to wash up before I check out the noise. As I come out of the kitchen, I see Patrick through the window. I quicken my pace to unlock and let him in. "I didn't know you would actually come!" I beam.

"Of course I came." He smiles, then brushes something off my cheek. "You're a mess." His face reddens as I giggle, shaking my head.

"Okay, put me to work, boss."

"Right, so, follow me." Heading back to the kitchen, I pick up a piping bag. "I'm currently decorating some cupcakes. Do you know your way around a piping bag?" He shakes his head.

"I figured as much, just watch what I do." I take the bag in my hand and swirl it around on the cupcake. "Now we just add some sprinkles and...voila." I smile at him and hand him the bag. "Your turn."

Patrick takes the bag and makes a sloppy blob on the cup-cake. Some of it is hanging off the edge of the cupcake and somehow on his fingers. He frowns and picks it up. "I think I may have messed this up."

I laugh and take the icing back. "Take that as your payment for tonight."

His eyes light up as he takes a bite out of the cupcake. His eyes go wide, "Best payment ever."

I laugh and ice a couple more cupcakes. "You can be on sprinkle duty, you can't mess that up. When you're done, just put them back exactly where I placed them. I'm designing the cupcakes altogether to look like a unicorn."

Once we finish, it's time to move onto the cookies for the baby shower. I grab the trays and start mixing up the icing to turn it light blue. "Hey Patty-uh, Patrick, can you put the cupcakes into the walk-in cooler?" The nickname slipped out before I realized it.

He smirks at me. "You called me that when we were kids, I don't mind."

I freeze, then spin around. "Wait- you're *that* Patty?"

His grin widens, "And you're Lizzy the Lizard."

Memories flood back and laughter bubbles out. "How did I not connect the dots? Oh my gosh!"

He shrugs at me and grabs the tray of cupcakes, "I knew it was a matter of time. Nice to be reunited, Lizzy." He says with a wink before turning to the cooler.

"So does your mom still make popsicles for all the neighbors?" I ask when I hear him return.

"Not since high school, man, what I would give for one of those."

"We can head to Sal's Drive-In to get some ice cream? Not the same as your mom's popsicles, but I wouldn't mind a cold treat."

"That sounds great! Let me put the last of the dishes in the dishwasher and we can head out."

As he does that, I put away all the food. "All I have left is some tarts that I will do in the morning! Let's get out of here." I grab my keys and walk with him to the door.

He smiles back at me and opens the door to his car. "See you there."

It's only a five-minute drive to Sal's, the whole way I thought about our childhood. I remember him giving me daisies every day. And he always wanted to play with my dog. I remember rainy days watching tv together and sunny days exploring the neighborhood.

Once I arrive at the drive-in, I move to sit at one of the tables outside. We both order burgers and joke about our childhood days under the flickering glow of lights.

Patrick orders a milkshake, and I watch him take a gulp of it. When he pulls it from his lips, there is a dollop of whipped cream clinging to the tip of his nose.

"Well look who's the mess now." I laugh, leaning across the table. Before I can process my actions, I swipe it off of him and plop it in my mouth. His face turns a bright crimson as I realize what I had done.

My eyes grow wide, but he turns back to me, a small sparkle in his eyes, "I just can't help myself when it comes to milkshakes: they're my favorite."

I realize my heart is racing, and I force a smile and nod back at him, taking a mental note of this information. We finish up our dinner, and I give him a hug bye, he hugs me for a beat longer than normal. I definitely didn't get away with the whipped cream stunt. "Thanks for the help tonight, you have no idea how much I appreciate it. I'll talk to you soon?"

He nods in agreement and we depart from the drive-in. Once I get home, I pour myself a nightcap before passing out while scrolling through Instagram and Facebook.

The next morning, I wake up in a daze but realize I was supposed to be at work thirty minutes ago. I don't have time to think about the dull ache in my back and speed off to the shop. Caroline has already finished opening chores and is working on this morning's muffins when I arrive. I throw my apron on and get to work with the tarts and box everything away. To stay focused and not think about my embarrassment last night, I put my AirPods in.

It's been about fourty-five minutes of working on the sweets when I feel a tap on my shoulder. I can't help but scream and turn around, my heart racing and I grip the counter. It was just Caroline.

"Oh my gosh, I'm so sorry. I kept calling your name, but you couldn't hear me." She hurries and says.

My heart is still racing, and I put a hand on my chest. "It's-It's okay. Just try to be louder next time, maybe? I am just-" I take a gulp, I'm safe and I'm at work. "Nevermind, I just scare easily." I force a smile out. "So, what's up?"

"There's someone here to see you." I look at the time, but it's way too early for any of the parties to pick up their food.

"Oh really?" I question and wipe my hands on my apron before heading out of the kitchen. I came out and was greeted by Patrick and a cup of coffee.

"Well good morning, Patty! What are you doing here?" I reach out for the coffee and wrap an arm around his waist. I quickly take a step back and have a sip. "Mmm pumpkin spice. Thank you so much, you are just too sweet." I hum and take another sip.

He smiles down at me and has that familiar hue tinting his cheeks. "I figured you could use a hand with deliveries. I know most of your clients are picking up but I would hate to ruin that beautiful unicorn we created." As he speaks, his smile keeps growing wider.

I beam up at him. "Well, that's awfully sweet of you, thank you!" I escort him back to the kitchen.

Patrick carries the cupcakes to the car with ease while I follow behind with my tarts. We pack everything into his car, and I triple check that it is all stacked safely. I decide to slide into the backseat to keep the unicorn cupcakes steady.

"So, I'm assuming you had nothing better to do on Saturday morning, so you decided to come help me."

He chuckles, shaking his head. "Well, I just didn't want all our hard work from last night to go to waste from one bad turn. It took a lot of blood and sweat getting those cupcakes sprinkled."

"Now, there's a passionate cake decorator if I've ever seen one." I laugh, surprised once more at how everything feels so easy with him. As the miles fly by, a part of me whispers that I don't want these days with Patrick to end. But the other part of me screams, I can't let myself get attached now, not after *everything*. I let out a sigh and his eyes meet mine in the rearview mirror. I hold his gaze for a second and then glance back out the window.

"Keeping me in line back there?" He teases, but I could tell his voice hints at something more.

"Oh...just protecting the unicorn! Precious cargo back here ya know?" I gently pat the box on my lap.

"Oh, I know." He responds and I feel warmth spread on my cheeks, I tore my gaze away once more, looking at the blur of browning fields outside.

The radio fills our silence, and he taps his hand on the beat to each song that plays. I focus on each beat rather than paying attention to the war going on inside me.

When we arrive at each house, he graciously carries everything for me as I finalize details with each customer. When we finish, he drives me back to The Flour Shop. Once he parks, I reach for his hand and give it a squeeze, "Thanks again for help-ing me. Not just today but last night as well. I'd be dreadfully tired if it weren't for you." For a moment he doesn't let go, but I pull away and slide out of the car. I give a quick wave as he pulls away and turn back inside to check on Caroline.

"Is that your boyfriend?"

"What? No, he is just a friend."

"Well, a friend would never just show up on a Saturday, to help with deliveries. You've done hundreds of deliveries, you can do it yourself." She states.

I roll my eyes, teenagers are always projecting stuff, I learned that from Katie. I make my way to the back and continue clean-ing up for the night. Once the kitchen becomes manageable, I let Caroline go home and I close up my shop.

As I speed home, I slow as I pass Gavin's house. There are a few lights on, and I can't help but wonder what Patrick is up to. But I stop myself from texting him, I need to sleep. And hopefully I can finally have a peaceful night of it.

# Chapter Four

## Patrick

I look at the time, I'm already running ten minutes late. Gavin is going to kill me for being late, again. I needed to get my morning coffee, and I have a craving for a cake pop from my favorite bakery. But first I needed to head to the store to buy some flowers. I buy a bouquet that has an assortment of daisy-looking flowers, some look light pink, others purple.

I set the flowers in my passenger seat and speed over to The Flour Shop. Caroline's attention moves to me as I come through the door, and she smiles as she helps her current customer. I wait patiently as she checks them and the person in front of me out.

I glance at the time, still ten minutes late, but that will change depending on how long I talk to Elizabeth.

"Lemme guess, you wanna see the boss?" Caroline smirks at me.

I lean against the counter, placing the flowers down on them. "How'd you know? Maybe I stopped in to see how you're doing?"

She rolls her eyes. "You're so lame." She turns to the back to get Elizabeth, who comes rushing out with a bowl in her hand.

"Hi Patty!" She starts stirring.

"He brought you those." Caroline points to the flowers on the counter, and I feel my face brighten.

Elizabeth's eyes soften and she looks at me, as she opens her mouth to speak, I quickly interject.

"I just notice you always have fresh flowers all around here, so I figured I would get you some."

She smiles at me sweetly, "Thank you, that's awfully thoughtful of you. I'm sorry Patty, but I have a bridal shower cake that needs to get done today. I'll see you later?"

I smile and nod. "Oh no worries! I am running late to work anyways, Gav will probably have a few words with me about that." I chuckle.

She nods and heads back into the kitchen.

"That was brutal to watch." Caroline is leaning against the counter, watching me.

It's my turn to roll my eyes, "Don't you have homework or something to do?" I tease.

"Nope! Homeschooled, I did it all this past weekend."

"Well...get me a cake pop. Thanks." I take out my wallet. I don't know why that was so awkward, maybe I crossed a line with the flowers?

Caroline places a bag with the treat on the counter and takes my card. "You know, she does talk about you. She likes all the help that you have offered."

I look at her and raise a brow, warmth filling my chest. "Really?"

"That's all the information I'm going to say. Employee confidentiality and all."

I can't help but laugh and shake my head, the teen gives me a satisfied smile.

～ele～

"Well, well, well. Right on time." Gavin drones when I walk in.

"I know, I know. I'm sorry." I place my backpack in my chair and pull out my laptop and files, placing them on the desk. "Is the client here?"

"Not yet."

I stop what I'm doing and look at Gavin with a raised brow. "What do you mean, I'm fifteen minutes late."

"Exactly, so I purposefully told you the wrong time so you would be here on time. Genius, right?" He smiles.

I shake my head. "I must be really bad then if you knew to do that."

"Well, if you wouldn't snooze your alarm so many times in the morning, maybe you would be on time. Anyways, here are all the quotes we are presenting to them today. Since you're the numbers guy you can run all that by them. I have to get out and buy more supplies, you got all of this covered?"

I look at the document that he handed me. "Yeah, I think I'm good. Sorry again about this morning."

Gavin waved me off and headed out the door. I took the time before the clients came in to create a presentation of their breakdown estimate. My phone starts buzzing next to me.

Elizabeth

> Sorry about earlier. It was a busy morning, thanks again for the flowers.

I'm about to type in a reply when the client comes in. I stand up quickly, glancing at the document quickly. "Mr. and Mrs. Dunn, it's so nice to meet you." I motion them to a chair and flip my monitor around to show them the cost breakdown of their kitchen remodel. I went over the timeline, permits, and everything they would need to know. After an hour of discussion, they sign a contract with me.

I quickly got everything put into our calendar so that I could schedule the contractors to begin work within the next week for them. Once I got everything scheduled, I picked up my phone.

> Hey sorry, I was in a meeting. No problem at all. Seems like we are both having a day.

> Tell me about it. I need to get back to this cake.

I place my phone down and try to focus on my work, but I can't stop thinking about what Caroline said, that Elizabeth talks about me a lot. I smile and hum to myself as I work, I finish scheduling the timelines for our crews and reach out to some of our contractors to ensure they have upcoming availability. I put on some music as background noise to help me concentrate.

By the time I get done with work, it's later than normal and I haven't heard from Elizabeth, so I pick up a burger on the way home. After I settle in, I hear a knock at the front door, Gavin and Stacey went out tonight for a date night so there could only be one person on the other side of that door. I'm already smiling by the time I swing it open.

"I've been waiting for you to come over for our walk."

"Sorry! I haven't been home long, so I ate and just got done. I should've texted you."

She nudges my arm, "I'm just messing with you. Let's go."

I walk out with her, letting her lead the way, "Did you get the cake finished in time?"

She nods, "Yeah, they had changed the pickup from yesterday to today. Which isn't a big deal, but it was a little stressful adjusting my timelines. They were extremely grateful, and the cake looks great! See look."

She pulls out her phone and opens the photos app. The cake was white with pink dripping down the sides and gold leaf brushed on. "It looks so elegant, you did a wonderful job!"

"Thanks, Patty." She hums while putting her phone into her pocket. "How was your day? You said you had a meeting?"

I nod and tell her all about the kitchen renovation I secured, in the middle of the story I hear shouting behind us. We both turn to see a kid, speeding down the hill on a scooter.

"Help!" He starts screaming as he is picking up speed.

I grab Elizabeth out of the way, but someone has to help the boy. I look around, there isn't anything I can grab, so I'm going to have to do it. I run up the hill to prevent him from picking up even more speed.

I time it out and jump towards him, spinning myself in the air so that when we go down, he will land on top of me. I hear the metal clank of the scooter as it hits the ground and skids down the hill.

"Are you okay, bud?" I look down at the kid jumping up.

"Y-yeah." He says clearly shaken. "Thanks."

"Carson!" Elizabeth runs up. "Oh goodness, are you okay?" She squats and starts inspecting the kid and nods when she sees there's no harm. "Looks like you're just shaken up. Maybe a free treat at my bakery next time you come will cheer you up.

The boy had big crocodile tears forming, he couldn't be older than seven. "Anything I want?"

"Anything you want." She nods.

He wipes his tears away with his fist and then takes off back down the road. I chuckle and shake my head. "That could have been really bad."

Elizabeth nods, "That was an incredible thing you did-oh! You're bleeding."

I look to see where I had rolled up my sleeve is now covered with blood. Now that the adrenaline is wearing off, I start to feel the sting. "Looks like it's just a scrape, I'll be fine."

She frowns and shakes her head. "Let's go get it cleaned up so you don't get infected."

When we make it back to her house, she rummages around the kitchen and comes out with a rag, hydrogen peroxide, and Neosporin. "This may sting a little." She pours the hydrogen peroxide onto the rag and places it on my arm.

"Ah!" I hiss as I feel it makes contact and starts to bubble.

"Sorry." She whispers and I look into her sad blue eyes.

"Don't feel bad, I'm just thankful you are taking care of me." I say softly to her. Her eyes linger on mine and then focus on my arm.

"Carson was extremely lucky to have had you. That must've been terrifying for him."

I nod back at her and place my hand on top of hers. "You seem kind of shaken, are you okay?"

She sighs but relaxes at my touch. "It's just been a long day." Her eyes meet mine and she places her hand on my cheek. "You are incredible. And so thoughtful. Between those flowers and saving Carson. I don't know how I got so lucky to have a friend like you."

I raise a corner of my mouth at her, "And I you."

# Chapter Five

*Elizabeth*

The morning rush has just ended, I'm going around wiping the tables off of powdered sugar when I hear my phone buzz on the counter. I choose to ignore it, I want the shop spotless so that I can start making some cookies. Plus, I can't stop thinking of Patrick saving Carson yesterday. It was so....attractive. Not to mention the flips my stomach did when he let me tend to his arm, it felt like those scenes in a movie. When he looked at me, part of me wished we were something more, but I can't entertain that thought

A few seconds later it vibrates again, and again. By the fourth ping, I stop my cleaning, wipe my hands on my apron and check the screen.



I shake my head and laugh. I haven't had a girls night in a couple weeks, I've had Patrick over every night.

Shelby



I roll my eyes and put my phone on silent. The chat starts going off, mainly Marie demanding more answers and Shelby messing with her. I finish cleaning the last table and start thinking about spending the evening with my friends.

Shelby is my nosey, gossiping friend that is always a constant mess. There is always something going on with her, she is also incredibly sentimental but tries to keep that a secret. She's a graphic designer, in fact she made all the graphics for my bakery. She also runs my Instagram account, I just send her pictures of my favorite creations, and she works her magic.

Marie is my always a step-behind friend. Most of what she says is laced with sarcasm, but she is incredibly caring and will show up when you need her. She is a high school teacher and is usually the one who demands girls nights; I don't blame her, if I only interacted with teens all day I would need time too. Both of my friends have been there for me since high school, and apart from Katie, they are my sisters.

If they are insisting on having a girls' night, especially Marie, I'm not about to argue. She has something she needs to tell us about.



The moment Shelby walks in with a bottle of Moscato and Marie carries in a giant bag of snacks, I know tonight would be good for me, the energy in my house shifts, and I feel instantly relaxed. I was busy right up until closing, so I rushed home and got the house ready for my friends. I still have flour in my hair, but they don't care. Girls night isn't about appearances, it's all about being cozy and gossiping. Which only comforts me a little, I'm out of my routine and desperately wanting a shower.

We curl up in my living room, candles flickering on the coffee table, blankets are piled on the couch, and the opening credits of some cheesy rom-com flickering on the TV. Marie lays out her spread of salty treats and dips onto the table, and I brought home leftover cookies, brownies, and some chocolate croissants.

As we set up the coffee table, Shelby pours the first round of wine. She walks in with three glasses, her grin is as mischievous as always. "Alright, Elizabeth. Spill. How's life with your new shadow?"

Marie nearly chokes on her pretzel. "Shadow? What shadow? Is this the guy??"

I roll my eyes, "Patrick. She means Patrick."

Shelby arches a brow. "Yes, and *Patrick* is practically glued to your hip."

I try to laugh it off, twirling the stem of my glass. "We're just... friends. He's sweet, and he hangs out at the bakery with me sometimes. That's all. Nothing worth gossiping over."

Shelby leans in. "Hanging out? Please. My mom saw you two on one of your nightly walks earlier this week. She said he looked at you like you were the last scone left in your bakery. And not only that, but Mrs. Higgins said she saw him helping with your deliveries one day."

"Shelby!" I groan, trying to fight the smile that tugs on my lips. I cover my face with my hands. "Stoppppp. I promise, we are just friends."

"Don't act like you don't enjoy this." Marie stated, leaning towards Shelby, wanting more.

"Uh-huh. Just friends who walk together every night." She continues. "Just friends who bring you wine and eat dinner here five nights a week. Do you know how long it's been since we've had a girls night? A whole month! All because he's here *all* the time."

I try to hide my smile but fail. The truth is, having Patrick around fills a part of my day I didn't even know was empty. But saying that out loud felt dangerous. And if I hint at anything more, these two are going to lose their minds.

Marie nudges me. "I don't know how I missed out on this part of town gossip. Elizabeth, you deserve someone who shows up for you. He clearly does."

Her words should have made me feel good. Instead, they twisted in my stomach. Blake had shown up too, showering me with flowers, kisses, sweet promises and always could make me smile. Until the day it all crumbled, leaving me with the mess I have to pick myself up from day after day. I look at the glass in my hand and take a sip, the Patrick stuff will definitely open the door for their questions again.

I force a laugh. "Anyway. Enough about me. What's going on with you two?"

Marie groans dramatically. "Dating apps are the worst. I swear every guy within fifty miles is the next big musician." She uses air quotes as she rolls her eyes.

Shelby snorted. "She's not wrong."

"But listen to this." Marie starts. "I finally found a guy that isn't a musician. He lives further out in the country. You would think: nice, sweet farm boy, right? Wrong! He wanted me to help with chores around the farm before our date! Can you believe that?!" She laughs.

Shelby starts to share her own stories and before long we are crying with laughter.

We spent the rest of the night laughing over horror-date stories, sipping wine, and randomly turning our attention back to the movie. Marie, the lightweight, stopped drinking after her second glass, Shelby after her third- but I pour myself one more. When I walk back into the living room, they are rereading cringy Bumble messages they've received this week.

By the time we make it halfway through the movie, Marie is asleep under the fluffy blanket, and Shelby is scrolling through her phone. I nurse my glass, staring at the tv, but my mind is elsewhere: Patrick. His smile, his patience, the way he looked at me sometimes like I was the only thing in the room.

I hated that it scared me more than it thrilled me.

The next morning, the smell of cinnamon clings to my hoodie as I drive down the familiar road to my parents' house. My hair is pulled into a messy bun, and I have a container filled with fresh cinnamon rolls sitting in the passenger seat.

Dad is already in the kitchen when I walk in. He is a dark-haired whirlwind in an apron, moving around the kitchen in a chaotic, yet still graceful, way. His pan is hissing and popping with the bacon loaded in it. He glances up at me, his eyes growing wide with realizations.

"Liz! Finally, my taste-tester has arrived!" He flips a pancake on the plate like the professional he is. "Try this, thinking of adding some pancakes to the brunch menu at the restaurant."

I laugh, setting the cinnamon rolls on the counter. "You're going to feed me before I even say hello?"

"Food is my greeting, sweetie. I'm surprised you haven't caught on yet." He shoots back, but walks to me, placing a kiss on my head and places a fork in my hand.

Before I can even take a bite, mom sweeps in from the living room. Her arm is full of binders that are bursting with pastel tabs and swatches. Her blonde hair is twisted into a perfect knot, and her blue eyes shine with her usual high-octane morning energy.

"Elizabeth, thank goodness. You have to help me decide between these ivory and cream linens before my bride has a meltdown."

I roll my eyes, what a normal morning in the Riley house. I smile at her though, grateful to see her. She places the binders on the counter, and they go sliding in every direction. She gives dad a kiss on the cheek as I look down at the swatches. "So? Ivory or cream?"

"Umm. Those look the same."

Both my mom and I shoot up and look at dad. "They're not." We say in unison.

I look back down at the binder and take a bite of dad's food at the same time. "Cream for sure, it flows with her pink theme. And dad- these pancakes are fantastic." I pull the plate in front of me and continue eating.

I look at my parents, I love the chaos of this house, more so, I adore the love that fills these walls. The way dad glances at mom when he's cooking, constantly wanting to be near her. He listens to her endless babble of wedding talk. And mom, she leans on dad for everything. He's her best friend and she has the "where you go, I go" philosophy with him.

It hits me suddenly why I stopped coming as often, seeing their love hurts. It's just a reminder of what I lost. I look back down at my plate and finish off the pancakes.

"Elizabeth?" Mom's voice broke through my thoughts, "Are you okay?"

I nodded quickly, forcing a smile. "Yeah, just...tired. Girl's night went late last night."

She studies me with those bright eyes that always see more than what I want, but thankfully, she lets it go. She turns back to her swatches, and I feel a twinge of guilt.

"Is Katie around?" I wonder.

Dad nods. "She's asleep. Last night was Homecoming, so she was out late. I don't expect her to wake up for another couple of hours."

"Well darn. Can you tell her to text me when she wakes up?"

"Woah, woah. Leaving so soon??" My mom states but they are both turned looking at me.

I sheepishly smile at them. "Yeah.. I have to do inventory this morning. I gotta place my order tomorrow. You understand right, dad?"

"Are you sure it's not to run off and spend some time with that boy Katie was telling us about?" Mom raises an eyebrow, and dad has a wide-toothy grin at me.

I groan, not them too.

"Yes, I have to go take inventory." I state. "And definitely tell her to text me after she wakes up. I have some things to say to her." What is with this town and gossip? "And before you ask. He's a friend. Nothing more, nothing less. Will you drop it?

My mom looks dejected, and I feel guilty once more. This time because I may have displaced my annoyance from last night and Katie on them. I sigh, "I promise I will come and spend more time later this week. I just wanted to bring over some cinnamon rolls, and if you want to ask about my *friend*, Patrick, then you can."

Mom squeals and kisses me on the cheek and starts to escort me out the door. "Sounds great! I can't wait! Oh! To have some time with my baby again. I'll see you then!"

It may only be Sunday, but this is going to be a long week.

# Chapter Six

## PATRICK

Most of my days consist of two things: work and Elizabeth. If I'm not stopping by The Flour Shop for a quick snack in between clients, I'm thinking about her. It's been almost three months since I moved to Nolensville, and somewhere along the way I stopped looking for a place to live. Moving farther than a few houses from her felt...impossible. But it has to be at some point, I can't stay at my friend's house forever.

We've fallen into a rhythm. Every evening, we go for a walk. Sometimes we talk about life, our jobs, or sometimes stroll in a peaceful silence. If I don't make it to her house by six sharp, she will be knocking on the door with that half-smirk that says, *what's taking you so long?* She knows by now that I'm chronically late.

Elizabeth is extroverted and always wants to be with someone. If I am unavailable, she will call either her sister or one of her friends to hang out with her.

I've learned Elizabeth's post work ritual: she has to have a glass of wine after work. But before that, she takes a shower to get off any of the sugar and stickiness that latched on at work. Her fridge is perpetually stocked to host a friend or two, or even ten. She typically cooks for someone each night of the week; and since I live nearby, most nights, it's me.

It didn't take me long to discover she doesn't like to be alone, she has someone over until she is ready to fall asleep. If I ever decide to go back home right after the walk, she gets a distraught look across her face. This always pulls on my heart, so I have long since adjusted my sleeping schedule and I make sure that all my work is done early, so that I almost never have to leave her before she is ready.

Today is different, her friends asked her to hang out, so she told me that I am on my own for dinner tonight. I have already started up most of my daily routine. I just parked outside the coffee shop so that I can get something to take along to keep me awake at work, and later I will look at some apartments in Smyrna.

The doorbell jingles overhead as I step inside, warming from the indoor heat. The chill of October has driven me to needing a hot drink. I get in line, but I can feel a set of eyes burning a hole into me. I try to ignore the feeling, no matter where I go in this town, someone is always watching, always whispering. Finally, I glance over and see Mr. Keller, the owner of the building Elizabeth's bakery is in, staring me down. I smile at him and order my coffee. But I feel that he is still looking at me, so I scroll awkwardly on my phone as I wait for my coffee. Once I get my drink, I turn to try to quickly head out.

"Patrick." His voice is rough, and he motions me with his worn hands to sit in his booth. He gave me a look that made me feel like I was a kid in trouble.

"Can I have a word?" He asks, though it doesn't sound like a request.

"Of course." I slide into the booth across from him. His arms are folded, resting on the table. He studies me for a minute, his look makes me want to hide somewhere.

"You've been spending a lot of time with Elizabeth."

I nodded. "Yeah. We've gotten close. She's—"

"I know what she is," he cut in, his tone soft but sharp. "That girl's been through enough heartbreak to last a lifetime. And we don't need some outsider making it worse."

Aside from Gav, no one has mentioned the ex. Hearing it spoken by someone like Mr. Keller gives some weight to how bad the breakup was.

I swallow, unsure what to say.

He leans closer, lowering his voice. "People still talk about her and...the ex. About how happy they were, about how fast it all ended. You weren't here for that, son, but we all were. And we all saw what it did to her."

I shift, heat crawling up my neck. "I'm not going to hurt her." I start to feel the challenge, this town doesn't want me to date her, but they don't even know me. "And I think everyone needs to realize, I'm not some guy she used to know. I'm the guy that's here now." I state.

"Intentions don't matter as much as the follow through does." His gaze hardened. "It's better to give up on any games that you're playing now, or else you will wish you weren't the new guy."

"I care about her," I state, a little louder than I intended. "More than I probably should. I'm not playing games."

For the first time, a flicker of approval crosses his face. Still, his warning hangs between us.

"Good," he finally said. He stands and taps his cane on the hardwood floor. "And one more thing, that girl hides more than she shows. Don't buy into the smiles and cupcakes show. You want to stick around? You better be ready to face her shadows. They're there, even if no one else sees them.

He leaves, the bell jingling again.

I sit frozen, my hand wraps tight around my cup, the heat warming my palm. I watch the steam and wonder if I have any right to want her the way I do. But at the same time, my heart swells with pride. I want to show them how well I can take care of her- how much I can be trusted.

I decide to stay at the coffee shop, Gavin is out at a construction site and I brought my laptop in from my car to answer emails and send out invoices when my phone vibrates next to me.

Gavin

Heard Keller cornered you. Everything good?

Is there no such thing as privacy here?

Nope, what did he want?

I set my phone down and run my hands over my face. I'm glad everyone is so protective over Elizabeth, she is worth protecting. I'm not the guy that ghosts girls or leads them on only to ditch them when someone else comes along. I just wish I was given a chance. By both- everyone and her.

A barista refills my coffee and I mutter thanks, I stare at my computer screen, seeing my reflection. I've always been cautious and tiptoe around everyone, that's what I have been doing since I moved here. But maybe it's time to be bolder, Mr. Keller ignited something in me; also, everyone judging me without knowing me, that just makes me want to show everyone who I am.

A voice pulls me from my thoughts, "Mind if I sit?"

It was Jake, one of the guys that we used for a roof repair a couple weeks ago. He slid into the seat across from me before

I could answer, his grin is lopsided but not unfriendly. "Heard Keller had some words with you."

I roll my eyes, "Word really does spread fast around here, doesn't it?"

He laughs and nods. "Yeah, but don't let it get to you. Keller did the same thing when I first started dating his niece."

I raise an eyebrow towards him, "And?"

"And I married her," he chuckles. "Everything has been fine ever since. He's like the town's grandpa, he loves everyone around and would take a bullet for them. As for the rest of the town...well you're the new guy and went straight for the town's sweetheart, they don't trust that. *Everyone* is rooting for her. Everyone wants her to move on and be happy. But it's hard to trust someone you don't know, and that's you."

He's not wrong, I haven't made an effort to get to know many people since moving here. "I guess I will just have to change that then." I say quietly.

Jake slides out of the booth and claps me on the shoulder. "That's the spirit. Personally, I'm on team Patrick. Just don't screw anything up, otherwise no one will let you live it down."

I sit back and start to feel lighter. Maybe Keller is just the voice of the town, echoing every doubt I have had since I first heard Gavin's warning. I focus back on my work, wanting to finish so that I can start coming up with ways to win the town on my side.

A week later, the cold morning air sends a chill down my spine as I help load Gavin's truck with tools and supplies. Keller's voice still plays in the back of my head, and I've made a decision. If I want them to stop looking at me as an outsider, I need to show up for this town.

So when Mrs. Green, who frequents The Flour Shop, mentioned to Elizabeth that her front steps are rotting. I offered to fix them for free. I pull into her driveway and immediately start getting to work.

By mid-morning, a few curious neighbors linger around, slowing as they walk by as I measure planks and hammer nails. I can tell they are talking about me with one another. I notice a few even looking and texting rapidly.

I keep my head down, focus on work, and not wanting to cause a bigger problem for myself. Besides, this would be good for our business. Since I am usually the one in the office, it's nice to get my hands dirty for once.

When I finish, I see Mrs. Green standing on her porch with a mug in her hand and her gray hair rolled in curlers. "I didn't expect you to actually come today, let alone finish in a day." She offers me the mug.

I wipe my hand on my jeans before taking it. "Well no sense putting it off, those old ones could have caused you some major harm.

Her eyes soften and she motions me to join her on a rocking chair on her porch. "A lot of kids your age will say they help and then forget. Speaks a lot that you actually show up." She softly rocks herself. "You remind me a lot of my son."

"Oh, where's he at?"

Her shoulders sag, "He died four years ago, in a car wreck." Her eyes tear up. "He would always be there for people that need it." She continues telling me about him; he was a star athlete in college and had just accepted a job for when he graduated. Then he moved up in the company quickly and started a family. Her sadness turned sweet in remembrance of him. I rock in my chair asking questions about him.

"Now, let's try out these new steps." I stand up and reach a hand out to help her out of the chair. Mrs. Green clapped when she tested the steps, her laughter carrying down the street. I caught sight of Mr. Keller across the street, his arms folded.

He had no expression on his face but gave a simple nod before turning and going back into his house.

I'll take that as a small victory.

"Well Patrick, thanks for the new steps. I really do love them." She sighs. "And thank you for listening to me. I misjudged you. I don't know what I thought of you before, but I see now you are just a quiet, gentle soul. People will catch onto that pretty quickly if you let them. And I'm sorry if I came off too harsh on you before."

I nod and thank her; her words stick with me when I drive back home.

A few days later, I had Jake help me patch up the church's roof. I helped Laken Henderson haul some heavy furniture to the dump. Little things have started popping up that people need help with. Word really travels fast around here. By the time November rolls around, strangers nod when I pass, more people talk with me in the coffee shop, and glances in my direction are less suspicious and more curious.

Gavin has noticed, too. "Making a name for yourself now, huh?" He says to me when he gets back to the office from a bathroom remodel.

"Just trying to make myself a better resident." I answer. And for the first time since moving here, I feel like this is truly starting to be home.

# Chapter Seven



*Elizabeth*

The day before Thanksgiving has been absolutely chaotic at work, and it is only eleven am. I have pies cooling on every counter, one of my 4 ovens beeps right on a schedule, and Caroline is answering the phone around the clock taking more orders for the upcoming holiday.

I wipe my hands on my apron when I feel my phone buzz in my pocket, I need to take a break anyways.

Patrick

Surviving?

I laugh despite the stress, he wasn't wrong. Plus, I love my job, and I love how everyone wants to use me for their desserts on Thanksgiving.

When the last customer walks out with her order that evening, I finally let out a deep exhale and fall back against the wall. My neck aches, and my apron is streaked with pumpkin filling and chocolate. My hair has been attempting to escape its bun all day, so I take it out and sigh in instant relief. I sit at the counter and stare at my phone, giving myself a break before beginning cleanup.

I purse my lips in thought, staring down at Patrick's name. A few days ago, the idea of inviting Patrick to Thanksgiving occurred to me. He is staying in town, so I know he could eat with Gavin and Stacey, but there is a huge part of me wanting to have him come to my parents.

My parents realize now that we are just friends, but there is that underlying message of bringing a guy over for the holidays.

But then again, he has been a huge part of my life for the last two months, and no one should feel alone on a day that is meant to gather with those you are thankful for.

Before I could second-guess myself, I typed.

So...want to have Thanksgiving with my family?

Three dots appear, disappear, and reappear once more. My heart pounded with the anxiety I have brought upon myself.

Patrick

I don't want to impose or take away from your time with your family.

Oh you won't be doing that all, they would love to have you.

You sure?

Positive. Bring your appetite, dad's a professional chef.

Then definitely count me in.

I smile, but part of me still is nagging. I hope I'm not sending him mixed signals.

❧ ❧

The next afternoon, Patrick walked over so that I could drive us to my parents' house. He carries out a pie that I made while I grab a container of cookies. On the drive over, I can tell he is nervous, he keeps tapping on his knee and adjusting his jacket.

"Relax," I tease. "It's just my parents, and you already know Katie."

He shoots me a look. "Just your parents, who are some of the most well-known people in the town. Your sister- I have no problem with her. But.." He pauses and I look over at him. "I'm just anxious to meet people for the first time."

I grin but don't argue, my mom will be sizing him up the second we walk in, regardless of our relationship status.

When we pull in the driveway, Patrick helps me by grabbing the pies out of the backseat. I hear a door slam and a small squeal.

"Bethy!!!!!!!!" Katie screams. I turn to see her speeding down the walkway toward me and pummels me in a hug.

"Hey Katie Cat!" I laugh and hug her back, thankful now for Patrick's help with the pies.

She lets go of me and looks up at my friend. "Hiya Patrick! I like the facial hair look." She turns back at me and raises her eyebrows a couple of times, causing me to roll my eyes.

I inhale deeply the second we step through the door, the scent of roasted turkey and herbs hit the moment we enter.

"Elizabeth!" Mom appears first, her hair is perfectly curled and resting on her shoulders. She wraps me in a hug before turning to Patrick. "And you must be Patrick." She has a sharp gaze as she takes him in, but she still has a welcoming air about her.

Patrick offers his hand, "It's great to meet you, Mrs. Riley."

She smiles and shakes it before ushering us toward the kitchen, where Dad is bent over a pot, his apron spotted with gravy.

"Smells incredible, dad," I state.

He turns to me, his face lighting up and pauses what he's doing to kiss my temple. Then his eyes land on Patrick. "So, this is the guy that Katie keeps talking about." His voice carries no judgement, just pure joy.

Patrick breaks into a grin, "Yes, sir. Patrick Williams."

Dad smiles back at him and then points to the wall. "Grab an apron, Patrick. You can help me finish the gravy."

Patrick's grin widens, and he does as he is told. He hops in with my dad, and they start talking as if they are old friends. I head to the living room and find Katie already munching on my cookies.

"Hey! Those are for after dinner!" I laugh.

My sister gives me a chocolatey grin. "Not when they are your cookies. Dad will eat them all." She takes another bite.

The rest of the afternoon unfolds more easily than I expect it too. Patrick continued to help dad finish dinner, and mom would randomly question him. Basic information, thankfully, about Texas, how his parents are, if he is dating anyone, if he has found a place to stay. He answered every question without hesitation and a smile on his face.

When we finally sit down, the table is picturesque for Thanksgiving. The golden turkey at the center of the table, mashed potatoes and cranberry sauce on its side, burnt broccolini, and mac & cheese. My stomach growls at the sight and smell of the room.

As we pass the dishes around, a thought hits me, Patrick fits in so easily here. Nothing about him today has been awkward, he has been his true, genuine self. He laughs at each of my dad's corny jokes, talks with mom about transfixing event spaces, and even indulges Katie in talks about cheer drama.

As Katie went on, I can't help but roll my eyes, she is upset that she was invited to a birthday party and a movie night at the same time. Unable to decide which one she should go to, Patrick nudges me under the table with his knee, and I glance over and smile at him. A playful smirk is on his face. A warmth spreads through me, and I feel my cheeks warm, I quickly look at my plate before my family or Patrick can see it.

After dinner, mom insists on pulling out photo albums. Normally, I would groan but tonight I sit quietly to the side and sip on a glass of wine. I watch as Patrick leans in close to see baby pictures of me with cake smashed into my face. He pays close to every story my mom says as she flips through the pictures.

As I watch, my heart starts to war with itself. Blake and my mom used to do this and laugh at the silly pictures of me, he used to help my dad cook and play games with Katie. My heart tugs thinking of how he fits in here. Patrick looks at me, and I force a smile, and something flickers in his eyes. I drink the rest of my glass and nod toward the door.

Patrick takes the keys to my car and brings out the leftovers. We say bye to my parents and sister, and he decides to drive us.

After a few minutes, he breaks the silence. "Thanks for inviting me. It means a lot."

I look out the window and nod, not wanting him to see the conflict I'm fighting. "Yeah," I whisper. "Me too."

# Chapter Eight

## PATRICK

Since Thanksgiving, things have seemed a little off with Elizabeth. The night was going so well, I absolutely loved getting to know her parents, she seemed like she was having a good time as well. I could tell she was trying to make sure I felt at home and included with her family. But since we left, she has been quiet. I'm starting to get worried about her, and I'm also worried that things aren't going to fall back into rhythm like they were before.

I'm sitting on the couch wondering about what I might do for dinner but also delaying the process hoping she might text me. I scroll aimlessly through my phone when her name finally pops up.



I grab my coat and drive to the liquor store and pick up a bottle of Cabernet and drive back. I walk into her house, no longer knocking because she keeps the door unlocked for me, and am greeted with the smell of Italian seasoning and garlic.

"Smells delicious," I call.

"Thank you, Patty! What'd ya get?"

"Your favorite." I hold up the bottle. Her eyes light up, she gives me a quick hug.

"You know me so well! Thank you!" She turns back to the stove and points to a cabinet. "You can just put it in there for me, thanks!"

I move to the cabinet and see that there were fifteen, no, maybe twenty bottles of wine. I start to close the door when something catches my eye. On the top shelf sits a framed photo, its glass cracked. I find it strange for a picture to be inside the cabinet, out of curiosity, I grab it. Elizabeth was maybe twenty and in the arms of a dark-haired boy. She's absolutely beaming, a smile I have never seen. The pieces click together- Gavin mentioned she was engaged. This must be him. But if it ended so badly, why would she still have a picture?

I'm still staring when her voice snaps through the air. "What are you doing?"

I turn, guilty. She snatches the frame from my hand, her eyes blazing with hurt and betrayal.

"I'm sorry I-""How about you don't go snooping in other people's things?" Her voice wavers. She tosses her spatula on the counter, kills the stove, and storms off. "I think you need to leave." She states before closing the door to her room.

I stand frozen, replaying the last sixty seconds. Everything happened so fast. Her mood changed so quickly. Her eyes... there was so much pain in them, it hurt me seeing her that way.

I wait a few minutes to give her time to calm down, and I head to her room. "Elizabeth?" I gently knock on the door.

"Go away!" Her voice cracks, swallowed by sobs.

What is happening? The breakup must have been bad if she is this upset about it *still*.

"Are you okay?"

"Go" she takes a shaky breath. "Away."

My hand lingers on the knob, but I can't move my feet to leave. I decide to go in, the door is unlocked and Elizabeth is sitting on the floor against her bed, her face buried in her knees. Her body is violently shaking. I sit beside her, and to my relief she leans into me as she cries. I wrap my arms around her and let her cry into my chest. I rub her back and I don't say a word. When she finally lifts her head, I brush her hair out of her face and wipe away her tears.

"I'm sorry," she whispers. "This isn't your fault. I-"

"You don't need to explain anything to me." I softly smile at her. "Just...tell me if you're okay.

She nods, but the smile she forces is paper-thin. She mouths 'thank you' and falls back against her bed looking up at the ceiling as a few stray tears run down her cheeks. "I ruined dinner." She frowns.

"It's okay. We can order DoorDash." I stand and reach out for her hand. She gives it to me and I pull her up. I walk her to the living room and give her my phone to place an order. I clean up the kitchen and throw out the overcooked rice and now-burnt chicken. I pour her a glass of wine and settle next to her on the couch.

She takes a sip and stares forward, I wrap an arm around her and gently rub her arm. I feel her begin to relax into me. For some reason, having her in my arms feels so right, and I realize all I want to do is make her happy, to feel safe, no matter what. We sit in silence, mainly because I don't want to upset her again.

When the food arrives thirty minutes later, I get up to bring it in. As I handle the food, she goes to the kitchen to get some plates and sits on the floor in front of her coffee table. I place the food out for us, it looks like she ordered an assortment of Chinese for us.

All I want to do is make her feel safe and like she can trust someone. It's clear to me now that she hasn't talked to anyone about the breakup. For her to have such a strong reaction to the picture, one she looks at every single day, it is clear to me she hasn't healed.

I'm raking my head for something to break our silence, anything to make her laugh, but I keep coming up empty-handed.

I'm forced to accept that small talk will ease the tension between us currently. "This is good."

"Mhmm." I notice she is pushing the food around on her plate, not actually eating anything.

"Are you wanting to watch a movie tonight?"

"I don't think so." She gets up and refills her glass. I sigh, wishing I knew what to do.

"I think I'm going to go to bed early tonight, I'm sorry." She lets out a sad huff.

"Don't worry about it, you need some rest." I state and she slowly nods. I take the dirty plates and wash them off in the sink. She curls up on the couch and pulls the blanket over her.

I walk over and grab her hand. "If you need anything, *anything*, I am here for you. Okay?" She forces a smile up at me and squeezes my hand.

Despite every fiber in me telling me to stay, I leave, feeling worry wash over me as soon as I close the door behind me. I walk home and sit on the couch, replaying the evening in my head. Gavin walks into the room and I guess he sees my expression. "You're home early and judging by the look on your face something happened."

I nod and turn to him. "What do you know about her ex?"

He shrugs. "They were together for several years. He proposed about two years in, and they were engaged for a year before it ended, just months before the wedding. She was, I think, twenty-three when he proposed, so very young. Like I said, no one knows what happened, and she has just been focused on work since it happened.

"And their relationship in general?"

Gav sighs, I could tell he doesn't want to tell me, but he knows that I won't stop asking until he does. He opens his mouth to speak but hesitates, finally deciding it's not worth a fight. "They were madly in love. They were the couple everyone looked at and wanted a love like theirs. They spent every moment together and if they fought, no one ever knew about it. They were just...happy."

"Since they broke up, everyone around town talks about how there will never be a perfect love like that. And I think Elizabeth knows that she won't love someone the way she loved Blake. That's why we warned you, Patrick. She's terrified. She's terrified to love again and she is even more afraid to lose it. Now, again, she refuses to talk to anyone about this, so it is purely speculation."

I nod and thank him before heading to my room. I stare at the ceiling, I think of her wine cabinet and the picture in there.

Not just that, but how many bottles of wine she owns. It made me wonder why she always wants to go buy more, most of them were opened, so would they have gone bad? I don't know, I'm not a wine person, so I don't have the slightest clue.

I decide to search for some good brands of wine to get one for her as a gift, and of course a few ads came up and next thing I know, I fell down a rabbit hole about functioning alcoholics. Some of the descriptions remind me of....

I feel a pang of guilt. Why am I doing this? She is heartbroken and had a rough night, and here I am about to diagnose her with an addiction. There are so many people that like to have a glass of wine to unwind at the end of the day. I throw my phone to the side and decide to get some rest. Just as I feel myself drifting away, I feel my phone vibrate.

Lizzy, you are going through something you aren't ready to talk about. I understand that, but I'm worried about you.

Don't be.

Just know that I am here for whatever you need.

It's been two weeks since that night. Elizabeth has returned to normal. For a few days after that night, she was quiet, only texting me a couple of times a day. When she came around, she brought me chocolate dipped pretzels as a peace offering. I had eaten them all by the end of the night. I guess she had just needed some space for a couple of days.

Christmas is in two days, so I am trying to pack at the last minute, like I always do. As I put on the sweater my mom demands I wear for our family photo, I hear a knock on the door.

"Yeah?"

"Hey Patty."

I quickly turn around, feeling my heart skip a beat. My face burns and my cheeks turn red. "What are you doing here?"

"Well, I wanted to see if you needed help with anything. I'm not going to see you for a few days. Gotta get my Patty time in."

We both laugh and she stands next to me, looking down at my suitcase.

"Oh that won't do." She proceeds to unpack my suitcase and then refold everything. I shake my head, but I don't dare mess with her perfection. I feel the heat once more when I see her picking up a pair of my boxers and folding them to replace them in my suitcase.

I busy myself by grabbing more clothes for her to pack, but she is unfazed by my clothes. Once she zips up the suitcase, I lead her back to the living room. "Are you excited to see your family?"

I nod, I'm not necessarily close with my family. My sister and I are just a year apart, but she lives in her own little world. We have gotten closer over the years, but we are still relatively surface level with each other. "My mom has apparently been running in circles getting ready for Christmas. We haven't missed a single Christmas as a family, so she is stressed with me coming so last minute."

Elizabeth nods, "What's she like?"

"My mom? Oh, she is incredible. She is always there for everyone. If someone passes away, she is the one organizing the meal train. She is the classic PTO mom, she volunteers for everything. She is always baking and hosting things for the neighbors. But when it comes to talking about things, I go to my mom. She is always a listening ear, even though she is a busy body."

"Dad is down to earth and I can easily talk to him, but mom just says what you need to hear." I can't help but smile. There's no place like home for the holidays, and I am excited to catch up with some sports talk with my dad, but I can't help but feel the longing for being away from Elizabeth.

"Well, they certainly sound amazing." She looks outside and her entire face lights up. "Look! It's flurrying!" She rushes outside and stands there looking up in wonder. I can't help but watch how excited she is. I laugh as she sticks out her tongue and tries to catch a snowflake.

We only stand outside for a few minutes before she states how cold she is and decides to make us some homemade hot chocolate. We head to her house, where she turns on one of the Christmas claymation movies. A few minutes into the movie, she jumps up from the couch and strides into the kitchen. I hear her rustling around in there before she pads back with a steaming mug and places it on the side table.

She settles in next to me and pulls a blanket over us, she fiddles with the blanket on her lap before blowing on the sweet drink to cool down. I start carefully drinking the hot chocolate and rest my arm around the back of the couch. I can tell she is transfixed by the movie as she starts to lean into me.

I'm glad she seems oblivious to everything when it comes to me, because I feel the heat on my face as I feel her weight shift onto me. I lean back into her until she is fully rested against me, my heart beats rapidly. My mind can't focus on the movie now that I have my whole world leaning against me. Everything feels *right* and now I have to leave tomorrow.

❦

"Patty" I hear Elizabeth whisper. "Patty."

My eyes shoot open and I'm trying to place where I am. I see her standing over me, oh my gosh- I fell asleep. I shoot up and feel anxiety and panic shoot over me. "Am I late??" I jump up and she puts her hand on my arm, instantly making me feel a tad calmer.

"No no, that's why I woke you. You need to get some food in you before you head to the airport."

I look around still in a daze, this was the first time I ever fell asleep here. "Oh my gosh I'm so sorry, you should have woken me."

She hands me a blueberry muffin that's still steaming from the oven. "Oh no, you looked too peaceful. I covered you up and made sure you would be comfy for the rest of the night."

I smile at her and take a bite of the muffin. "Well thank you. I guess I didn't realize how comfortable your couch is. I feel rested- and my back doesn't even hurt." I place my hand on my lower back and stretch. "Well, I better get going. I'll see you when I get back?"

A small frown appears on her face, and she gives a small nod. Elizabeth takes a large step towards me and wraps her arms around me. I quickly wrap mine around her and rest my cheek on top of her head.

"Travel safe, okay?"

I nod and pull away to look down at her. My eyes fixate on her lips. Every nerve in me is screaming *kiss her*. But what if it's the wrong move? She just had that breakdown a couple weeks ago, and all the warnings from my friends from the past 3 months play in my head, constantly making me question every touch, every little moment.

She tilts her head to the side, "What is it, Patty?"

I shake my head, torn from my thoughts, and my eyes meet back with hers. "Oh nothing. Just thinking how much I'll miss those pastries of yours." I smirk and she playfully punches my shoulder, making me chuckle. I give her a quick hug again. "Okay, okay. I'll be safe. See you in a few days."

I walk back home and Gavin takes me to the airport, of course he had a whole interrogation about me sleeping over at Elizabeth's. Once he realizes that nothing happened, I look out the window as he speeds down the interstate. I am already counting down the minutes until I can get back to see Elizabeth again.

# Chapter Nine

*Elizabeth*

Christmas this year was absolutely wonderful. My dad outdid himself with the Christmas ham and all the sides. Mom came over and "helped" me back, which meant she came over to stay out of dad's way. I didn't ask for anything this year, but they got me more things to cook or bake with. Katie got a new phone and some outfits, she was already showing off her new pajamas and hoodie to all of her friends over Facetime.

I go home and turn on the tv and pour myself a glass of wine. I fall asleep at the light of the tv and the exhaustion that Christmas always brings.

The next morning comes too early. I'm not expecting to be busy, but I am quickly proven wrong. Most of the customers are burnt out from hosting out-of-town relatives and come in to buy assorted pastries all morning.

Now it's two o'clock, and I haven't had a customer for hours. I long since cleaned up the kitchen and have been idly sitting and playing on my phone. I have no major orders right now, since everyone had placed them all for Christmas. So I decide to go ahead and close up early, I deserve a break.

Once I get settled back in at home, I realize how quiet it is. I'm following my same routine but can't figure out why for a while until it occurs to me, Patrick is always here. I sigh and shoot a text message to some of my friends to see if they would want to come over. As I wait for a response, my finger hovers over Patrick's name. I go ahead and click on it.

I laugh at myself and see that Shelby texts back and will come over shortly. I start prepping a small charcuterie board and as I finish up, I hear a knock at my door. I hurry and let her in from the cold and walk her into the living room.

"I was kinda shocked that you reached out, with it being the day after Christmas. I thought you would be comatose by now."

I nod in agreement. "I know. I closed the bakery early today, but when I got home, I got bored so quickly." I admit.

"Well... guess what! I got a small raise at work, not much, just three percent, but hey, money is money!" She grins and flips her blonde hair over her shoulder.

"Oh my gosh, that's amazing!" I curl up on the couch and she plops down next to me.

"Yeah! Anddd..." she pauses dramatically while her lip curls up a bit. "I'm dating someone."

"WHAT?! Tell me everything! What's his name?"

"His name is Daniel, he's in marketing. We have been dating for around three weeks. We matched right after our girls night and went out on our first date a week later. But we decided to take it slow because of Christmas and we didn't want to put any pressure on ourselves with expectations during the holiday season." She shrugs.

"So now that Christmas is over, we will see what happens. But he is amazing, so far he has checked all the boxes." I can tell she is truly smitten by him, that smile on her face is a big tell-all.

"What about you and Patrick, any progress in that field?"

I raise my eyebrow. "We are still just friends, remember I don't want to date?"Shelby raises her eyebrow at me suspiciously, I can tell she is holding back something, but she ends up not saying anything and pops a cheese cube in her mouth instead. After chewing the cheese, she turns back to me.

"Well in my opinion, I think you two would be great together. And if you are already spending so much time together, you know you would get along great. Plus, everyone in town is starting to love him! He is such a sweetie!"

I sigh and nod. "I'll keep that in mind." And I wave it from my thoughts immediately. I already know what it feels like to lose someone, and I'm not going to risk Patrick too.

We ended up watching *How to Lose a Guy in 10 Days*. By the time the credits roll, I'm half-asleep. Shelby quickly leaves and I head to bed.

Two days later, I'm pulling the last set of cookies out of the oven to cool. "Elizabeth! Customer!"

I sigh and shake my head, I have so much to do: cleaning today's mess, organizing a baking schedule for the current New Years orders, and planning out what I want to serve tomorrow; so why is Caroline needing me to address the only person in the store? I throw my oven mit down and head to the front.

I first see the dirty-blonde messy hair. I gasp and launch into him.

"Patty!" I wrap my arms tightly around him. "You're back early!"

He hugs me back and laughs. "Yeah, I was actually craving one of your chocolate croissants, so I decided to come back and get one. But *Caroline* here says you're all out." Caroline sticks her tongue out at him and continues to play with her phone.

I roll my eyes, teenagers.

"Well, what a shame. I guess a muffin will just have to do." I pick one out of the case and hand it to him. "I have a few more cookies to decorate, and I'm sure you need a nap. Wanna come over later and catch me up on your trip?"

"Of course, see you then." He gives me one last hug and heads out the door.

I head back to the kitchen and keep prepping things tomorrow. I only have a few orders to deliver tomorrow, but the day after I will be slammed with New Years orders. I hum to myself as I finish up everything, Caroline helps me finish up the shop and we head home. I take a quick shower and grab a bag of chips to snack on until Patrick shows up.

Eventually, I hear him outside so I run to the door to greet him. When I open the door, he is holding a small present tied with a red bow and a bouquet of daisies.

"Aw Patty," I gasp, taking them. "You shouldn't have. Do you have wrapping skills that I don't know about?" I giggle.

"My mom always recruited me to help wrap my sister's presents growing up." He chuckles and watches me tear open the gift. I tear open the gift and laugh at the hand towel inside that reads: *Texas' Best Baker.*

"This is perfect," I grin. "Thank you." I point to a box under the tree. "That's for you."

He smiles as he unwraps the scarf and beanie set I gifted him. "Wow, thank you! I love them!"

I smile back at him. "I've noticed how cold you are on our night walks, even though you don't complain."

"That's sweet of you, wow thanks. I really do love it." He hugs me tight and then he grabs all the wrapping paper to throw it away. When he sits down next to me, I move to face him and bury my feet under his leg. "So how was your family?"

"They're great." He beams. "My sister is moving to New York in a couple months, so my parents are thinking about moving out here since it will be close to me and closer to her."

He shrugs. "I don't think they will do it, they have gotten settled in Texas, their whole life is there. It would be different if they were ready to retire."

"Would you want them to move here?"

"Well, it would be nice, but I don't have a preference. We used to eat together once a week and I miss that time together, but I have also loved having my own life here."

I nod in understanding. Ever since the breakup, I've been distant from my parents. Mom worries nonstop about me. I keep myself busy with work, and they will stop by occasionally to check on me. Now that I think of it, it was until just before Thanksgiving that I didn't come over to see them. Things are changing, maybe Patrick...I shake the thought from my head and focus back on our conversation.

"Well either way, I am happy to have you here." His cheeks flush light pink and he smiles at me. I pull the book I had been reading off the coffee table and start to read. Patrick pulls a blanket over top of us and starts to play on his phone. I realize I missed our companionable silence. It was nice finally having a normal night at home after a week and a half of being alone.

⚘ ⚘

New Year's Eve has arrived, and I am coated in all kinds of sugary substances. I have been in the bakery since 5am, so that I can get everything done for all the parties going on tonight. I have baked 400 cookies and am in the middle of frosting them when I hear someone coming into the kitchen.

I glance up to see Patrick, handing me a coffee cup. "I got you a white chocolate mocha. I had a feeling you are having a day."

"Oh, thank you." I eagerly take the drink and sip it. "Mmm. Yeah, I needed that."

"I also came to help." He pulls off his jacket and hangs it on the coat rack. He walks back to me while rolling up his sleeves.

I can't help but smile, this guy has to be the most thoughtful man I have ever met. I nod towards a stack of pans. "All those should be cooled off and ready to clean."

"Yes ma'am." He gets right to scrubbing the pans and puts everything back to where it belongs.

Thanks to him, and the mountain of dishes that disappears, I am able to get all the orders done a lot quicker. In fact, I am able to make some dough for some pastries to sell later this week. Caroline handles the customers coming in for pickup. I send her home once there are only a few left, so that she can hang out with her friends for the holiday.

"So," I turn to Patrick once she heads out. "Any plans for tonight."

He smirks back at me, "Not unless you're asking?"

"Well, the girls are getting together at Marie's, and I was wondering if you would like to come?"

His smile widens, "I would love to."

I try to swallow my excitement; I have been hoping for a chance for him to meet my friends.

"Well, let's get everything cleaned up so we can go get ready."

When we arrive at Marie's you can hear the music and laughter spilling out of her house. We walk through the door, and Marie instantly sees us come in, she runs over and places a glass of champagne in both of our hands. Her dark curls bounce as she throws her arms around me.

"Elizabeth!" She squeals and then glances again at Patrick, really studying him. "So, this is the famous Patrick."

Patrick grins, charming as ever, and reaches out to shake her hand. "I hope only the good stuff."

"Depends on your definition of good." Marie teases with a wink.

Marie decorated her house with glittery steamers and string lights draped on the walls. Shelby is deep in conversation with a tall, broad-shouldered guy I don't recognize. She beams when she spots me and runs to us, tugging the guy with her.

"Elizabeth! This is Daniel!"

Daniel offers a polite nod, and I catch the way his hand lingers on her lower back, her cheeks flushed. Seeing her so happy softens something inside me.

Shelby's eyes dart to Patrick and light up. "This must be Patrick!" He starts to reach out to offer her his hand, and she shakes her head. "Nope, I'm a hugger!" She fully embraces Patrick, and he laughs when he makes eye contact with me.

Patrick slips naturally into conversation with Daniel when Marie pulls me to the side. Shelby notices and steps over.

"I didn't know you were bringing a *date*." Marie states excitedly.

"And don't say any of the friends crap, Elizabeth. We can see now how you look at each other. I swear you even blushed back there." Shelby pipes in.

I open my mouth in protest and look back at Patrick. "I don't want to get into it. He's just...he's Patrick. And it was about time that he met you both, so I thought why not tonight?"

"On the night that ends with a promised kiss?" Shelby questions. "Yeah right."

"You guys." I groan and look back at Patrick. He does look so handsome, and I love the way his eyes crinkle when he laughs. A blush rises to my cheeks and both of my friends squeal. They push me back over to Patrick.

Marie gets into an instant conversation with him, and he is able to keep up with her quick wit. I can tell he is proud of himself, when he glances over at me and I give him an approving nod. I manage to get a laugh out of Daniel, who is incredibly kind and put together, is exactly what Shelby needs. I find myself soaking in the moment, all my friends are in one room. And for once, all the jagged edges of my life are smoothing out.

The night slips into a blur of games that Marie threw together, snacks and teasing laughter. Marie insists on playing charades an hour before midnight, and we all were several glasses into the champagne. Patrick tries, and fails, to act out *The Little Mermaid*. Shelby and I nearly cry laughing as he moves and wobbles his way around the room.

It's my turn when Shelby suddenly shouts, making me jump and spill my champagne on me. "It's almost time!" She jumps up and grabs another bottle of champagne and frantically fills each of our glasses.

Marie turns the music into a background hum, and we all gather around the coffee table. When we hit the last ten seconds, we raise our glasses and Marie starts the countdown.

"Three, two, one- Happy New Year!" We all cheer and clink our glasses together. Patrick turns to me with his glass up and I freeze when our eyes meet. Before I can overthink, I lean forward and my lips brush his cheek. "Happy New Year, Patty." I say softly.

His smile turns into a boyish grin as his cheeks turn bright red. "Happy New Year, Lizzy." He says back.

For a moment I feel like we are the only people in the room, I don't think of the past and what's been lost. I just think of what it could be.

# Chapter Ten

*Elizabeth*

A couple weeks later, I'm working by myself. It has been a slow day, so I am by myself in the shop. January is always slow from all the fitness New Year's resolutions and people taking a break from sweets after the holidays. I'm wiping down my counters and humming to myself when I hear the bell over the door jingle.

"Afternoon, Elizabeth!" Mr. Keller's voice fills the bakery.

I look up with a smile, "Hello, Mr. Keller! Come on and warm yourself up. Braving the cold for a slice of lemon pound cake?"

"Oh, you know me so well." He chuckles as he walks up and leans on the counter, his cheeks and nose pink from the crisp winter air.

I plate the slice of cake and slide it over to him. "Do you need an apple strudel to go for Margaret?"

"Oh no. She joined the resolution train and is trying to eat less sugar. She's trying to make me join in with her." He rolls his eyes. "I could never, your cake is too good to give up."

"So what you're saying is, she thinks you're out running errands, but you wanted to cheat on your new diet?"

He erupts in laughter, "Don't spoil our secret!"

I wink at him, "You can trust me. In fact, that slice is on the house."

"Well thank you darlin', now there is something I've been wanting to ask you about." He takes a hefty bite of the cake.

"Oh? What's that, Mr. Keller?"

"That new boy in town? I've seen both of you spending quite a bit of time with him."

I take a breath, but feel my cheeks flush as New Years flashes into my mind. "That's not a question Mr. Keller."

He chuckles a bit, "Yeah, I guess so. Is he treating you right?"

I feel my entire face heat up and I nod. "Yeah, he is." I tuck a strand of hair behind my hair. "Patrick's different. But in a good way, you know? He's kind, he listens to me...I trust him. Plus, I think Mrs. Green has a thing for him." I say with a chuckle.

"Oh yes, she hasn't stopped talking about those stairs Patrick built her, that's for sure." He shakes his head. "I just want to make sure you're good. I don't want to see you get hurt again...you know, like before."

I drop my eyes to the counter. "Yeah..." I look back at him. "I'm good. Patrick is good."

Mr. Keller takes a bite of his cake and studies me for a long minute. "Remember, the best people come into our lives when we least expect it. They can fix things we are unwilling to fix, and they can bring light into our darkness. Don't be afraid to see what's in front of you because of fear that stemmed from the past."

I nod, his words sinking into my gut. Patrick has brought light into my life. "Is that what Maragret did for you?" I continue cleaning up while Mr. Keller finishes his cake.

"Oh yes, and she did a lot more. If you can believe it, I was a grumpy young man. When I came home from the war at twenty, I had seen things that people don't even want to hear about. I watched my friends- my brothers die. My Margie, she brought light into a very dark world. After we got married, she stayed up with me when I had nightmares. She is a blessing."

He wiped his mouth with a napkin, "Well, thanks for the company darlin', I best be getting back to Margaret before she gets suspicious. See you soon!"

I wave bye to him and cut off the kitchen lights, deciding to go home early since today has been so slow. I'm about to walk out when something outside catches my eye. I walk to the window and see a man in a brown hoodie, brunette hair and about 5'11. My heart immediately begins to race, and I run to the back to hide. I find my phone, which feels like it weighs about a hundred pounds. I call Patrick.

"Hello?" His voice is cheerful but instantly shifts when he hears mine.

"C-can you come get me?" My voice cracks, and I only now realize my cheeks are wet.

"Y-yeah! Where are you? Are you okay?" I can hear the worry in his voice, and I hear his keys jingling in the background.

"At work please hurry." I sob.

"Okay, just breathe for me. Tell me what's happening-"

"Just hurry." I end the call before he can finish. My phone slips out of my shaking hands as my knees give way, and I col-lapse to the floor. I draw my legs to my chest and bury my face into my knees. A few minutes later I feel arms wrap around me and I jump in fear.

"Shh. It's just me." My body relaxes when I hear Patrick's voice and I lean into him. "What's wrong?" His tone is steady, but thick with worry.

I shake my head, "I-I." I try to take a deep breath. "I saw someone- I think it was-" I cut myself off. "You won't get it."

"Try me. Who'd you see?"

I stare at the floor, avoiding his eyes. "No! You won't think of me the same. Please...just take me home." I start to push myself off the floor, but I still feel weak. I glance out the window one more time and the guy is gone. My hands and body are still shaking, I grab onto his arm to one: steady myself and two: to feel his protection. I follow Patrick to his car and he drives me home.

"I'll have to get someone to drop me off at work tomorrow." I whisper.

"Don't worry about that. Let's just get you home."

When we get home, I head to the wine cabinet and take out a bottle, Patrick comes up from behind and gently slides the bottle out of my hands. "You don't need this, let me get you a glass of water. You need to rehydrate."

I narrow my eyes at him, "Give me the bottle, Patrick."

"Elizabeth..."

"Hand it over." I demand.

I watch him carefully as his shoulders eventually slump. "Fine." He sighs and gives it to me.

I turn back around and pour myself a glass and quickly drink the entire glass. I refill it and head back to the couch where Patrick is now sitting, frowning.

I sit down and cover myself with a blanket, a few tears still rolling down my cheek. I wipe my face with my sleeve. Pointless, because the tears are still forming. "So...what was that about? With the wine?"

"I just think you need some water. And you just went through something, bad it seems. So I don't know if alcohol is the best choice."

My eyebrows furrow, "Well it's not hurting, and it's helping me to calm down."

He slowly nods, but I can tell he doesn't agree with me. "Are you going to tell me what happened?"

"Nope." I stare at my glass and swirl the red liquid around.

He stands up suddenly and starts pacing.

"Patty?"

He takes a deep breath, runs a hand through his hair, and then drops back onto the couch beside me. After a beat, he turns quickly and takes my hand into both of his.

"Elizabeth, I am worried about you. From the way you reacted from a picture and now this. I get a phone call from you crying and then see you completely petrified. Do you know what it's like to see the person you lo...Please tell me what is going on. You know you can trust me. Don't let this be another thing you bottle up. What happened?"

As I listen to him, I feel guilt engulf me. I haven't wanted to burden him with worry like everyone else, but that look in his eye twists my heart.

Tears sting my eyes. "I-I'm okay." My go-to line, when anyone asks. Just like everyone else, he doesn't buy it. But everyone else has left it alone when I give that answer.

"Don't give me that lie, Elizabeth. You aren't okay, even now you still have tears soaking your face. Talk to me." He pleads.

I stare at him and then turn quickly away.

"No!" My voice cracks, "Patrick! No! You won't see me the same! You won't get it! Now leave it alone, please!" I start sobbing into my hands, I feel him staring at me for a long pause and then I feel his arms around me.

A dam has opened up and I cry in his arms, falling into his chest. He takes the glass from my hand and fully wraps his arms around me, holding me close and rubbing my back. When my sobs turn into sporadic sniffles, he pulls me away and tilts my head so that I look at him.

"I'm sorry. I won't push you into talking to me again. I just...I- yeah. I'm worried about you, and I care about you. I just want to make you happy."

I nod, "I know." I take a deep breath and look up at him. "I'm fine." It's a lie, but it's all I can manage right now.

Patrick studies me for a second then takes out his phone, "You're not cooking tonight, I'm ordering a pizza. I think you have earned a junk food night."

"Perfect." I smile and rest my head on his shoulder. "I'm glad I have a friend like you."

# Chapter Eleven

## PATRICK

I walk home, worry weighing down every step. The further I get from Elizabeth, the more I want to turn around and sit with her. But she keeps pushing me away.

"Hey Pat." Stacey calls. "You ran out of here in a hurry earlier."

I force a smile towards her, but she realizes something's up.

"Pat? What's wrong?"

I open my mouth to start about everything that has happened in the last four hours, but I quickly close my jaw. This is

Elizabeth's business, and I don't even know what is going on. Just that she saw someone.

"Just a rough night." I state and head into my room.

I lay on my bed and think about tonight's events. I have never seen her so...scared. She ended up drinking a whole bottle of wine that night, and there was nothing that I could do to get it away from her. But who did she see? And why does she think I wouldn't understand? Was it her ex? It would have to be, but I thought he was gone?

Ever since the turn of the year I started thinking that there might be a future between us. I haven't had the guts to ask her out, but there have been more flirtatious glances from her, and little touches exchanged here and there. A touch on the arm, on the small of her back. But that could all be ruined now, especially if she saw him.

Anytime we take a step forward, something makes her go two steps back. I run my palm down my face and grab my phone to unsilence it, just in case she calls. She was pretty tipsy when I left, but I made sure she made it into bed so that she wouldn't hurt herself.

As I start falling asleep, I make a promise to myself to not push her, she trusts me enough to call me for help. But maybe it's time I stop hoping for a future between the two of us.

Two nights later, Elizabeth asked me out for dinner. It was clearly a peace offering. I didn't text her much yesterday, only to make sure she was good and she kept assuring me she was. She went to work as normal, and I stayed available, just in case I got another phone call like the one I received yesterday.

I'm staring at the menu when all of a sudden, I feel a finger poke the spot between my eyebrows. "You got your worried face on. What are you thinking of?"

"Oh-uh-nothing." I quickly state. I know she isn't going to let up so I have to think quickly of something. I did overhear Stacey and Gavin talking about having kids soon, so I know they will want me to move out to convert the guest room into a nursery.

"Tell me Patty." She frowns.

I fixate on the cuff of my sleeve, rolling it up. "I just have to get the ball rolling on finding a place to move. I'm about to overstay my welcome."

"Oh."

I can tell she bought it, plus it isn't *technically* a lie. And I don't need to tell her about my conflicting feelings about us.

"So, I'm looking at some apartments in Franklin, of course it isn't Nolensville, but it is the same distance from work."

Her eyes remain focused on the flickering candle on our table.

"Move in with me." She blurts.

"What?" I sit back.

"Yeah, move in with me." Her eyes meet mine and she smiles. "You are already over all the time, I have an extra bedroom for guests that never come over. So might as well be yours." She shrugs.

"I-um."

She leans in closer to me, "At least think about it."

I nod, as much as I would love to live with her, my love for her would make it difficult. What if she starts dating someone? I couldn't handle that. But I could at least take care of her and make sure she was okay. "I...I'll think about it. Thanks."

The next day I'm sitting in the living room drinking my morning cup of coffee. I recently posted an opening for a new carpenter for our business, so I'm reviewing applications to find someone when Gavin joins me.

"Find anyone good yet?"

"Nope, but I still have twenty more to go through today, hopefully we'll have a couple of potentials by this weekend."

Gavin nods and pours himself a cup of coffee and joins me in the living room.

"Can I ask you something?" I say as I close the laptop.

"Shoot."

I push my laptop aside, "Elizabeth asked me to move in with her."

Gavin pulls the mug away from his lips quickly, causing some to spill onto the floor. "Nope! Don't do it. That's a bad idea."

"But-"

"No, you are in love with her, and she only sees you as a friend. Even if things have been changing like they have recently, it's still a roller coaster. It's only going to hurt you, and what if you find someone else? You can't bring her there."

"I'm not going-"

"Pat, you are going to have to. Yes, she may have kissed your cheek on New Years, but there have only been some flirty conversations since then. She keeps showing you that she doesn't want to be anything more than friends. Besides, when anyone asks, she is adamant about that fact... But ultimately, it's up to you. If you want to live with her, fine, but if you or her start seeing someone else you have to move out."

I sigh, I know he is right, but I just can't shake the feeling of being there for her. I nod and look back at my laptop. "Thanks, I will keep that in mind."

I open the computer back up and get back to reviewing the applications. Gavin leaves for a client's house and I start to hum to myself as I work. Eventually I close the laptop, but I can't get up. I just feel that I have to move in with her, not because of my feelings but because of her.

But after both breakdowns she has had, I really don't think she should be alone. Yes, I have been feeling conflicted, but despite that I still have undeniable feelings for her. Gavin is right too, if she were to start seeing someone else, I wouldn't be able to bear to watch that. I sigh and pull my phone out of my pocket.



I begin my search for apartments and get a few narrowed down. I will be able to get a tour booked for two of them tomorrow. As much as I feel like I need to take care of her, I'm not her boyfriend, *just friends*, her words repeat in my head.

~ele~

The first apartment I tour has everything I need, so in just two weeks I will be moving twenty-five minutes away. Which isn't so bad, but maybe this separation will do me some good. I need to put some distance between myself and Elizabeth.

I feel like her boyfriend, but without the title or any of the benefits. As much as I love spending almost every day with her, it's hardest when I find myself wanting to kiss the top of her head when we hug or run my fingers through her hair when she leans against me.

As hard as it is to resist those impulses, I know her heartbreak is harder. So putting space between us will help me, and then maybe it will help her too: to heal on her own without using me as a distraction.

The apartment isn't anything extravagant, but it has a big window that provides a ton of natural light. The walls are a clean grey, and there is a ton of potential for me to build the space up. I start ordering furniture for the space, and have my parents send me a few of my old things. Once I buy the major necessities, like a bed and dresser, I close out the tab and sit back in my chair, rubbing my tired eyes.

I glance at the stack of resumes on my desk. I need to prepare for interviews, but I can't stop my mind from circling back to Elizabeth.

I wonder if she'll miss me, or if she'll even notice that I'm not there. Will she call me as much to hang out? Or will this have the opposite effect and she retreats even more? I shake my head, I've got to stop worrying.

I read through several resumes and reached out to some potential candidates and set up some interviews. If anything, I am learning that life continues on.

—ell—

I'm pacing through my living room, waiting for Elizabeth to come over. I invited her to check out the place now that I'm all moved in. I also cooked dinner for her, I want to impress her for some reason. I feel like this is the first chance that I can show my intentions. I lit candles throughout my apartment, and I waited for the knock on my door.

When she arrives, she holds out a fluffy blanket. "I got this as a housewarming gift."

"That's thoughtful, thanks Lizzy!"

She walks in, throwing her coat on the couch, she begins wandering curiously around. "This is a nice apartment, nice job Patty!" She continues to walk around when she notices the dinner table topped with steak, mashed potatoes, and asparagus. "And you cooked."

I feel my stomach doing flips and I lead her over to the table. "I wanted tonight to be special. What would you like to drink?"

"Whatever wine you have will be fine." She waves her hand.

I shift my weight, "Um, I don't have any."

Her eyes narrow, "Really?"

I wasn't expecting this type of reaction. I nod and slowly sit down next to her. "I guess I didn't think this through…"

She stiffens and pulls away from me, "Think what through Patrick? You're being weird."

I reach to her lap and grab her hand. "I'm only saying this because I care. But Elizabeth, I think…I think you may be addicted to alcohol."

She snaps her hand out of mine and stands up. "What are you talking about?! I'm not addicted! Why do you keep bringing this up?"

"Well look how you're acting." I gesture at her. "You have so many bottles in your cabinet, you drink more than one glass a day, and every time you're upset you run to it. I think you've gotten dependent on it to help whatever it is you're going through!"

Her eyes burn into me, other than that one night, I have never seen her look so angry. "How dare you judge me, it's none of your business how much I may or may not drink! You aren't me, you haven't been through what I've been through!"

"You're right, I haven't...but you refuse to talk to me! I'm not judging you, I'm trying to help you. But you refuse me any time I try to help. It's like you only want me to make you feel better! I want more than that, I want the good and the bad!"

Her eyes widen. "What did you say?"

"I said, I want you for the good and the bad." I grab her hands. "Please?"

She yanks her hands out of mine and shakes her head. "No, you don't know what you're asking of me."

She grabs her coat and storms out of my apartment, slamming the door behind her. I run after her

"Elizabeth!" I call, but she is already down the hall. This time I chose not to chase after her. I close the door and walk to the second plate of food, I throw it in the trash. I haven't felt this angry in so long. I don't know why every time I see her ends up with us being pushed further apart.

# Chapter Twelve



*Elizabeth*

Ever since our fight two weeks ago, a part of me feels…empty. Patrick has long since apologized to me, but I don't know how to move forward. His words were so close to what Mr. Keller said. Now I take my walks alone every night, so I have replayed our fight almost every night for the past two weeks. He came in yesterday to buy a pastry, and it was so awkward. I didn't want to apologize yet either, he really overstepped this time. I should let him in, but it is so hard, so *scary*.

Obviously, I can't hang out with my friends every night, so things have changed back to how they were before he knocked on my front door. I go home and have a glass of wine, feeling some apprehension each time I pour a glass.

My house is quiet now. But not the same type as before. Before it was suffocating, I couldn't make it out of my grief. Now I am filled with longing for *him*.

I notice some habits I've formed since he moved here. Every other day he would stop by for a cinnamon cake, so I would have an extra set out for him. So now, I have several sitting in my fridge at home, for whenever everything turns back around. When I'm cooking at home, I keep glancing over at the couch to look at him. Only he's not there.

Now, I'm sitting on the couch, nursing a wine and begging for his name to pop up on my phone. I'm wearing a hoodie he left over long ago. I sink deeper in it, inhaling his fading scent. My heart aches at the thought of him.

I realize I relied on him more than I want to admit. He became an anchor for me, he brought light into each day and was an escape from my past. Now that my anchor is gone, I'm lost in the waves.

I take my last sip and head out for my walk. Shoving my hands into the hoodie's pockets as I walk out the door. A door closes nearby, and I instinctively glance a couple doors down, hoping to see him. Instead, I see Stacey.

"Hey Elizabeth! Going on your walk?"

I nod. "Yeah, care to join?"

"Sure! But let's make it a short one, it's freezing!" She walks towards me, and I meet her in front of my house.

"So, how's the interior design life going?" I ask, trying to make small talk. Even though we have been neighbors for a few years, I haven't gotten to know Stacey as well as I've wanted to.

"Oh, it's good. And your bakery?"

"Good." I nod awkwardly.

Stacey nods back and lets out a breath, a cloud of breath from her lips. "Listen, I came out hoping to talk to you.""Oh?" I say, caught off guard.

"Patrick really means a lot to Gavin and me. And I know everyone in town is starting to see what the three of us see. But he has such a kind soul, and I don't want to see him hurt."

I nod, seeing where this is going. "He does have a kind soul, and I don't want to hurt him."

Stacey stops abruptly and turns to me, shoving her gloved hands in her pockets. "Then what are you doing, Elizabeth?"

"I-uh," Her assertiveness makes me shift on my feet, "I don't know. Am I hurting him?"

"Well, he decides out of nowhere to up and move out. He doesn't come over here anymore for your walks. Now it's been almost a week without any contact from him. And the only thing I can think of is something happened.

You know, he took off in a flash a couple months ago, came home hours later and was acting weird. Elizabeth, every time he has been upset it's been because of you." I could tell she is getting angry, and guilt digs its claws into me.

"I know the whole town is just wrapped around your finger, but Patrick is *our* friend. And he cares deeply for you, and while everyone is busy protecting you, I need to protect him. I know you had your broken engagement, broken heart, blah blah blah. But Patrick- he isn't the guy that plays with girls-"

"I'm sorry, I-" I try to interject.

"No, you need to listen. Because he is going to continue on with this unless you make a definitive move. And it's long past time. Either try things with him or let him go. You can be friends but allow him to move on." She finishes and lets out a huff.

I fight back the tears in my eyes. "You're right. And I'm sorry. I needed to hear that." I let out a breath, releasing some tension inside me. "You're a good friend, Stacey."

"He's like a brother to me, and I just want to see him happy."

I nod in agreement. "I want him to be happy too." A corner of my lip curling up.

She raises an eyebrow at me. "By the look of that smile, it looks like you have an answer?"

"Yeah," I softly admit, "I do."

# Chapter Thirteen

### PATRICK

A couple hours into my workday, I'm discussing some upcoming appointments with our receptionist, Carly, when the door opens and a blonde walks in. Her darting eyes show confusion as she looks around the lobby. Carly is about to say something, but I decide to intervene. "Afternoon ma'am, is there something I can help you with?"

She smiles at me and tucks her hair behind her ear. "Yes, I just moved into an older house, and I want to renovate it. One of my friends recommended y'all."

I nod and motion for her to follow me to my office. "My name is Patrick by the way."

"Becca."

"Nice to meet you, Becca. So, what do you want done to your place?" I sit at my desk and pull different folders, getting ready to show her pictures of the jobs we have done.

"I would like to completely revamp my kitchen, living room, and my bedroom to start." She pulls out her phone and shows me some pictures.

"Okay, so I think this type of setup in the kitchen, with the beige base color everywhere is the type of vibe I am going for with my house. Got anything like that for the bedroom?"

I nod and start pulling up the pictures of bedrooms we have completed in the past and searching for some most similar to the picture she showed me. To fill the silence I ask, "So are you new to the area?"

She nods. "Yeah, I just decided to get a fresh start with life, and this is my first step towards it."

"I understand that I just moved here a couple months ago myself. I only knew my business partner and his wife. I have always loved Nashville and Middle Tennessee in general. I hope you grow to enjoy it, too."

Her face lights up as I speak, "I know absolutely no one. I've felt so outcast that I decided to do these renovations so I can start to feel at home."

I frown, "Hey, me and my friend are getting dinner tonight, would you like to join us so you can't say that anymore?" Elizabeth had sent me a text last night asking for us to go to dinner. And with how welcoming she was with me, she would love to help Becca feel at home.

"Oh, that would be lovely."

I give her my card, "Okay just shoot me a text and I'll tell you where we're going. Anyways, let's get to talking about these renovations. I'll have to get one of the contractors out to survey and get an estimate. So, let's continue discussing your goals and budget."

After around forty-five minutes of discussing her ideas for renovation, I finally had enough information to send out to a contractor to get an estimate. I escort her out of the office and grab my phone out to text Elizabeth.

Three dots instantly appear on the screen, disappear, and reappear.



Once Becca texted me, I told her the time and place. I couldn't help but feel bad for her. I'm sure there is more to the story of her wanting to start her life over.

# Chapter Fourteen



As I closed up the shop, I couldn't help but wonder who this surprise guest that Patrick is bringing, I'm assuming Gavin is tagging along. But surely Stacey would have updated him about our conversation last night. Unless she didn't want him to spoil the news.

I head to the diner and pick a booth for the three of us. I see the door open out of the corner of my eye and in comes Patrick, I start to smile, my heart racing. I realize he is holding the door open for a girl, my heart plummets, and my smile does the same. I have to force it back up and stick my hand out to her.

"You must be Patty's friend. I'm Elizabeth."

The girl gives me a side smile and looks between Patrick and myself. "I'm Becca, nice to meet you."

I feel a pang of jealousy as he looks at her. I sit down and try to swallow my feelings as I look at the menu. This is exactly why I didn't want to have feelings for someone again.

Patrick slides into the booth next to her, "Becca just moved here and doesn't know anyone. So, I figured she can start hanging out with us."

I nod, "Oh of course! So, what do you do?"

"I'm a musician." *Of course she is*; everyone moves to Nashville to work in music. I have to force myself not to roll my eyes.

"And I own my own online boutique that generates a lot of money to give me the freedom of making music." She shrugs a bit and then turns to Patrick. "I found more pictures of things that I would like to do to my house."

"Oh, let's see them." He leans into her and looks at her phone. They talk about renovations for a while as I feel myself sinking further into myself. I feel like an outsider at this booth. Eventually Patrick brings up my bakery.

"So, did you have a lot of Valentine's orders this week?"

"Oh yeah, mainly chocolate dipped strawberries. I offered those last year and it was a huge hit. I also had a few cakes and cookies." I nod.

"You work in a bakery?" Becca questions.

"She owns one," Patrick beams. "And she is an absolute magician in the kitchen."

I feel myself blush and make eye contact with him, "I saved you some cinnamon cake, it's at my house when you come by next."

I can't help but observe Patrick. Has he been going to spend time with her? Is this why Stacey came to have that talk with me last night, as a last-ditch effort? Is he dating her? I feel jealousy burning inside me. Becca is nice, and he deserves to be with someone like her. Maybe it's for the best that he moves on, I haven't been able to open up to him fully, after all.

I think about Stacey's words. He is nice and wouldn't ever hurt me, but I was dragging him along. He put me first all these months, I need to put his feelings first. If he likes a girl, then that's great, he deserves it.

I try to tune in to their conversation, but they are so engrossed in each other, talking about uprooting and places to see around here. I stare back down at my plate and dab a fry into ketchup.

At the end of dinner, the three of us walk to the door. Once we get to the entrance, Patrick hugs me bye and then turns to Becca. I step outside and head to my car, I hear them laughing and I turn to see they are a few steps behind me still. Her hands are shoved in her jacket pockets as he walks her to the car. I fight back the tears that sting my eyes and dart for my car.

When I get home, I curl up on my couch with my glass of wine. I turn on the TV, but I don't select an app, I keep it on the Roku home screen. I sit in silence as I think about what happened between me and Blake. Now my newest fear is happening, I'm losing Patrick. A sob escapes me and I cry into his hoodie that I left balled up on the couch last night.

❧ ❦

A month has gone by, and I have seen Patrick only a few times. A huge part of me resists the urge to text him. He found someone, and I took too long to come to my senses. I don't want to get in the way of his happiness, and I definitely don't want Stacey to come after me. I still miss him like crazy, and my heart yearns for him. I don't even get as excited for work as I used to, he hasn't stopped in for weeks now.

I lazily get ready for work and head out. On the way to my car, I tie my hair in a messy bun. I turn on the radio, but it's just white nose. My mind is filled with the to-do list for work.

Wedding season has officially passed now, so I only have to worry about a few small birthday orders. Before I do that, I need to start prepping batches of pastries for Caroline to be able to make over the weekend. I decided to take the weekend off since the birthday cakes will be picked up today. I am thankful to be alone today, I won't have to deal with Caroline constantly asking where Patrick is.

As things are in the oven, I take the time to clean up the store when I hear a customer come in. "Welcome in, what can I-" I turn around and see Becca standing there. "Hi Becca, what brings you in?"

"Well, I remember you telling me about this place and Patrick raves about it all the time. I just finally decided to come and try." She smiles and comes to the case to look at my options.

"So um, do you talk with Patrick often?"

"Oh yeah, all the time. He is so nice." She lets out a giggle, this only confirms for me that they are seeing each other. I don't feel in the mood to press any further. She orders a blueberry muffin and leaves. I watch her head across the street to a coffee shop. Right when I start to look away, I notice Patrick's car pulls up so he can join her.

I gasp and turn away, a pull in my heart. I hurry into the kitchen to put all my attention into creating more brownie batter, not caring that it is splattering all over me and the counter. I should be happy for him, for both of them. He is *very* attractive, sweet, and just...*perfect*. I guess I just assumed he would wait around, or not date at all. Man, I am awful to expect that of him.

As I'm stirring, I feel a hand on my shoulder, and I let out a small yelp and turn around. Patrick is standing behind me with his perfect smile, "Sorry, didn't mean to scare you."

I force a smile at him and look away, I'm suddenly angry and I have absolutely no reason to be, he came in here after all and not the coffee shop.

He grabs a stool and sits by me. "I haven't heard from you in awhile. Is everything okay?"

I nod and pick the bowl back up to continue stirring. "Yeah, just busy."

He leans onto the table. "I understand...it has just been awhile. Can we hang out soon?" The image of him and Becca pops into my head, and I have to push it away.

"Yes of course. When would you like to?"

"I was actually thinking I would hang out with you until you close up and then we can go to get some dinner?" I look at the time, it's about thirty minutes until closing, I hadn't realized how quickly the day has gone by.

"Okay, is Becca going to be joining?" I glance at him quickly.

He shifts uncomfortably, and his face turns that familiar shade of pink.

"No? It's just us." He reaches out and puts his hand on my arm. "I miss you."

I can't help but smile back at him, my heart skipping a beat at his touch. That smile melts all the anger towards him away. He raises his thumb to my cheek to wipe off some batter, I can't control the heat that fills my cheeks at his touch.

"I miss you too." I whisper, staring into his eyes. I quickly turn away, not wanting to complicate things further. "Okay, let me get to cleaning up. You know the drill."

He helps me with washing some dishes as I bag the batter for tomorrow's brownies. We clean up and I leave a note for Caroline in the morning about everything she needs to make. I head out to my car and Patrick goes to his.

"Are we going to your house?"

I nod.

He grins at me and jumps into his car and waits for me to pull away before following me. At a red light I get a text.





I smile, I love how thoughtful he is. I roll my window down, sticking my arm out to give a thumbs up. I glance in my rearview mirror at him and see his grin from ear to ear.

I leave the door unlocked in case he comes over before I'm done with the shower. I take one as quickly as possible and hear the front door close just as I get out. I hurry and get dressed and join him on the couch. "What are you wanting to eat?" I say as I braid my wet hair.

"I'm in the mood for sushi, would you like that?"

"Oh, that would be amazing! Let's go!" I throw a hoodie on, not realizing it's his, since I've been wearing it for the past month. I shove a beanie over my head to try to protect it from the cold, which won't be too successful with my wet hair. I turn and look at him, his face is bright red, I raise an eyebrow his way.

"I've been looking for that hoodie." He states.

I look down quickly and back at him, my eyes going wide. "Oh- I can give it back."

"No, no. It suits you." His smile softens. We stare at each other for a beat and then he holds his keys in the air. I follow him to the car, and he drives us ten minutes to the restaurant.

I can't help but feel the butterflies in my stomach, so I reach to turn on the radio and start to hum along to the music. I find that I don't know how to talk with him and he is being just as awkward. He keeps shifting uncomfortably in his seat. I take a deep breath, I know we are more than whatever is going on.

"So, Becca?"

He looks up quickly at me. "Yeah?"

"She seems nice."

He nodded again. "Yeah, she is." His eyes focus back on the road ahead.

I nod, I absolutely hate this. Why can't he just admit they are dating? We sit in silence for the rest of the drive. Once we sit down at the restaurant, I glance at him as he looks at his menu.

"Eliza-"

"Patr-" We say at the same time. "Go ahead."

He takes a deep breath. "Elizabeth..I." A blush was growing across his face. "I'm going to be flying back to Texas in a couple of weeks. A family friend of mine is getting married and I haven't seen her or anyone else in years. So, I was wanting to have some company and I-I was wondering if you would like to be my date?"

I can't help but smile and nod, a little too eagerly. Relief washes through me. "Of course, I'll be your date, Patty."

His smile matches mine and he reached across the table to squeeze my hand. "Thank you. Now what were you going to say?"

"Oh nothing-just. Um, so why didn't you ask Becca?"

He raises an eyebrow. "Not to be rude, but why would I?"

"Well...aren't y'all dating?"

His face turned bright red, "Oh no. She just got out of a bad relationship. That's why she moved here. Plus, she isn't my type, I'm into brunettes." He blushes again and looks down at the table.

I feel something burst within me. I bite my lip and look at the menu, trying to hide my joy.

After a brief silence he looks back up at me. "Is that why you haven't been talking to me?"

"I-um-maybe?" I fumble with the words to say, "You moved and you kept saying you were having to work, I thought you just were using that as a code word to not make me mad."

He shakes his head. "I will never lie to you. Listen, if I ever start dating someone I will tell you. Okay? But that isn't on the forecast right now." He lets out a breath. "Are we okay now?"

I nod. "We are good. I'm sorry for not reaching out to you this past month. I'm sorry about lashing out at you when you were trying to take care of me...both times. I got scared I was losing you." Should I tell him? No, my brain almost can't keep up with the change of events. I need time to process everything. Texas would be the perfect time to reveal my feelings.

He reaches across the table to grab my hand, causing my stomach to flip.

He smiles at me and gives my hand a squeeze. "Don't worry. You can't get rid of me that easily." I beam back at him.

He lets go of my hand when the food arrives. I feel so relaxed being with him again. Things are finally back to normal. When we finish, I walk outside only to be greeted with a huge drop in temperature. I shiver and he puts his arm around me. "I'm assuming you once again didn't check the weather?"

I shake my head, "The weatherman always lies. And it's always so unpredictable!"

He laughs and hurries me to his car. As he drives me back home, it starts to snow.

"Wow, I really misjudged today's weather." I laugh. As soon as he parks, I jump out of the car and look straight up, twirling in the snow. I look back at Patrick, "I guess you need to get going. Between yesterday's rain and this amount of snow, the roads are going to freeze." I frown, not wanting to say bye yet.

"No, I need to catch up on my missed time with you. Let's go inside." I can't help but smile as I grab my keys from my purse.

Once inside, I went to the kitchen to make some hot chocolate for the both of us. When I make it to the couch, he already has a blanket ready for me to snuggle up in, and *Harry Potter and the Chamber of Secrets* turned on. I give him his drink and wrap the blanket around myself and lay on the couch with my legs on top of his.

At the end of the movie, I grab both our mugs and head to the kitchen to put them in the sink when I look outside.

"Well, it looks like we may have a whole Harry Potter marathon tonight." I feel bad for being selfish and not sending him home, but there is no way I will let him drive with the roads covered with snow.

He gets up and joins me at the window. "No, I can make it home, it is all just on the road, there is probably hardly any black ice."

I shake my head. "No, I can't let you chance it. You're staying here tonight. And I don't want to hear an ounce of protest."

He opens his mouth in response but quickly shuts it. I smile triumphantly and we head back to our spots on the couch.

I turn on the next movie and sit next to him this time to not trap him under my legs. He puts his arm around the back of the couch as he normally does. I smile to myself as I realize for the first time how warmth radiates from him. I close my eyes and take a deep breath, inhaling the scent that I missed so much. I force myself not to hum in bliss. I focus my attention back on the movie.

"I missed you, Patty." I whisper.

"I missed you too, Lizzy." He responds softly. He drops his arm around my shoulders and pulls me close. I welcome the closeness and rest my head on his chest. I feel my eyes get heavy, but I don't want to move.

<hr>

A few hours later, I wake in my bed. I guess Patrick carried me in here at some point in the night. I look at my clock, it's 3:30am. I decide to get up and get a glass of water and I find

Patrick asleep on the couch rather than in the guest bedroom. I tiptoe to him and cover him with a blanket.

Temptation gets the best of me, I can't help but run my fingers through his hair, "I don't deserve you." I whisper and continue to the kitchen for my water and head back to bed. I quickly fell back asleep, finally getting a nice *restful* and nightmare free sleep for the first time in a month.

When I wake up in the morning, I can hear Patrick moving around. I pad out of my room and am greeted with the mouth-watering smell of bacon and eggs. "Well look who decided to take my job." I laugh.

He chuckles, "Good morning. How did you sleep?"

"Fantastic, you know you didn't have to carry me to my bed."

"I know, but I just figured you would be cramped on the couch."

I shake my head at him. "Why didn't you go to the guest room?"

He shrugs at me, but a smile tugs on his lips as he looks at the food he's cooking. "I don't know, I was comfortable I guess."

I can't help but smile, I join him in the kitchen and put on a pot of coffee for us to enjoy. For the first time in years, I feel my life is finally back on track. I think I can make this my new normal, this can be what I can look forward to the rest of my life. In Patrick, I have found simplicity. Not some perfect romance, but a normal routine. This is what movies don't show, a simple life in which you can love and be loved. Patrick shows up for me and doing these simple things, well it makes my heart grow. I didn't realize it until now, but every little thing he has done for me has helped me to believe in love once more.

# Chapter Fifteen

## PATRICK

In the past two weeks, it seems like everything has changed for the better. Elizabeth seems a lot lighter, happier even. I have fallen more in love with her and I'm pretty sure, for real this time, that she has feelings for me too. She has started sitting closer to me, finding reasons to be near me, laying her head on my shoulder.

But the biggest change: she has started showing up to my office, bringing me and everyone else treats. Because of how long it has taken us to get here, I don't want to push it. I'm letting her take her time, and I'm letting her take the lead. I have started going on walks with her several times a week now, reminiscent of how it all started.

We are on the plane to Dallas, and she's watching Netflix on her iPad, occasionally glancing out the window. I've been using this time to get caught up on work documents. Right when the pilot announces that we are in descent, she takes her headphones off and turns to me.

When we land, we head to baggage claim, Elizabeth goes ahead and finds our carousel as I start looking for my mom. I see her standing near an exit and hurry over to give her a hug.

"Hi baby!" She gives me a tight squeeze and a kiss on the cheek. "Where is she?" She whispers. I feel my face go red and nod towards Elizabeth.

"She's getting our bags, come on." I lead my mom towards Elizabeth, and she quickly gives her a hug.

"It is so nice to finally see you again, Patrick talks about you all the time." My eyes grow wide, she may be a problem and spill too much information.

"Elizabeth," I cut in, "this is my mom."

Elizabeth smiles back at her, "It's a pleasure to meet you as well. Thank you for picking us up.

"Of course, sweetie, now y'all get your things and let's get home."

We did as we were told, and my mom spent the whole ride chatting about all the things going on at home.

"Well unfortunately, Catherine won't be able to make it in from New York; her flight was cancelled. She is on the standby list for a flight tomorrow, but it doesn't seem like it is looking good for all of us to be together again. But! That means you don't have to sleep on the couch, Patrick! Elizabeth can take Catherine's room."

I feel disappointed, I really want my sister to meet Elizabeth. I think they would get along so well, plus having her approval means the world for me. But my parents' couch isn't the most comfortable object to sleep on, and I was dreading that.

When we pull up to the house, I see Elizabeth looking at it with wandering eyes. "So, this is where you grew up." She smirks at me.

"It sure is." I smile back. "You aren't going to snoop through all my things, are you?"

She nods excitedly, "Now how did you figure that out?"

"I just know you too well." I wink at her. I get out of the car and grab her suitcase out of the trunk and carry it in for her. I escort her to Catherine's room and let her settle in.

As I head back to my own room, my mom grabs me. "She's beautiful, and she seems...right for you." I smile down at my mom. "I can see why you have been so infatuated with her.

"Thanks" I beam, "Thanks again for driving us, I'm going to get settled. Is dad meeting us for dinner?

"Yes, he has to finish up at work.

I knock on the door for Catherine's room, and Elizabeth swings it open. "Hey," I smile softly at her. "I just wanted to show you the layout," I point to the door right across from hers. "This is my room, and the one on the left is the bathroom."

She looks up at me with sparkling eyes, "Thanks, Patty. I'm going to go ahead and start getting ready."

"Okay," I say softly.

Once I get unpacked, I decide to change into something a little nicer for dinner and open the door to my room. After a few minutes she comes to my room and is holding two shirts. "Which one? The blue one or the black?"

I look at the two quickly, "Blue." I state with no hesitation. I have always adored her in blue.

She goes back to her room and returns when she is done. She has done her makeup and curled her hair. I have never seen her so dressed up, she is breathtaking. I'm even more excited for her to meet my dad now.

We head off to a fine steakhouse, and my dad orders wine for the table. I notice Elizabeth hesitates before reaching for her glass to take a sip. She quickly eyes me and I look away.

"Now, Elizabeth, do you think I get to try your cinnamon cake that Patrick is always rattling on about?" My dad questions.

"Sure, I just have to go to the store to-"

"Oh, don't worry about that! Just give me the list of ingredients and I will run for you." My dad interjects.

My mom swats his harm. "Oh honey, she's on vacation! Don't make her work. Sorry, Elizabeth. Both of these two have no self control when it comes to their sweet-tooth."

Elizabeth giggles and shakes her head. "It really is no problem at all. I would love to cook for y'all especially since you opened your home for me."

My parents look at each other and smile at each other, I know this is the moment that Elizabeth won them over. I feel my chest warm, and I can't help but grin at the girl sitting on my right.

⸙

Dinner with my parents went perfectly. My dad kept giving me winks throughout the evening to give me his approval, now the only thing left is to actually win her heart. At the wedding in two days, during a slow dance, I plan to confess my feelings to her. I feel excitement and nerves. What I think about the most is finally holding my world in my arms. I want to stare into those beautiful blue eyes and lose myself in her gaze.

I lay down and start to fall asleep, willing for the next day to come, when I hear a soft knock at the door. I get up to see what Elizabeth needs. As soon as I open the door, her arms are wrapped around me.

I rest my chin on top of her head. After a few minutes, she pulls away and looks up and she smiles gently. "Thank you for bringing me. I had a lot of fun tonight."

"I'm glad you came."

"Goodnight Patty." Her eyes stare up at me. I can see something that I have never seen reflected back at me. Her breath catches and she takes a step back.

"Goodnight." I whisper.

She takes a few more steps back and closes the door behind her. I didn't realize until her door clicks shut that I was holding my breath. I step back toward my bed. Why didn't I just kiss her? I look back at her door and at my bed. I take the two steps back to her door and knock on it.

She quickly opens it, "Yes?" I close the distance between us, placing my hand on her cheek and I lean down to kiss her. I feel her body relax into mine and her hands rest on my waist as she kisses me back. After a moment, I pull away and rest my forehead against hers. She giggles and grabs both of my hands, interlocking our fingers. I don't think I have ever smiled so hard in my life.

"You have no idea how long I've wanted to do that." I whisper.

"Me too." She whispers back. "Goodnight Patty." She stands on her tiptoes and kisses me again.

I collapse on my bed, smiling from ear to ear. I don't think I have ever felt this happy. I replay the last minute in my head and drift off to sleep.

# Chapter Sixteen



*Everything is dark, I try to run, to scream. But there is no escape. Where am I? Suddenly, dark brown eyes seem to envelop me, his voice is all around me.*

I shoot up, tears streaming down my face. I try to take note of my surroundings, I'm in a strange bedroom. Then I remember: Patrick. I scurry out of bed and across the hall into his room.

"Patty," I whisper. He is deep asleep, I nudge his arm. "Patty." I say again but feel my voice crack.

His eyes open sleepily, but when he notices me by him, his focus hardens. He sits up and grabs my hand.

"Elizabeth," he says quickly. "What's wrong?"

"I had-" I choke back the tears, "I had a nightmare.""Oh sweetheart." He pulls me down onto the bed with him. I lay my head on his chest and begin to cry. I feel his arms tighten around me. His security makes me feel anchored to him. Everything starts to feel better.

"Do you have them often?"

I nod. "Almost every night."

His arms tighten around me, I close my eyes and listen to his heartbeat. I start to feel more relaxed, he kisses the top of my head.

"I thought tonight would be different. I finally..." I trail off.

"You finally what?"

I look up at him. "I finally went to sleep happy."

His eyes search mine for a moment and he pulls me up to kiss me. I feel the same butterflies I got earlier tonight. He cups my cheek and wipes away a tear with his thumb.

"Do you want to go watch a movie to take your mind off of it?"

I shake my head. "I don't want us to be up all night." I lay my head on his chest, "Being right here is helping."

❧ ❧

I wake up to movement beside me, a soft moan escapes my lips as I feel a kiss planted on the side of my head. I open my eyes to see Patrick smiling at me.

"Good morning."

"Good morning." I say with a stretch. I sit up and look at him. "You kissed me last night."

His smile brightens, "I kissed you last night. And I'm going to kiss you right now."

He starts to lean forward, and I smash my palm to his mouth. "No! I have morning breath!" I jump out of the bed and dart out of the room.

I hear him laughing, I look back at him as he is rushing up to get me. I run smack into his father, and I can feel my face heat.

"Woah, slow down there!" The man bellows.

I feel Patrick come up behind me, placing his hand on my lower back. "Morning dad, do we have anything I can cook for breakfast? Or should I go out and get us food?"

"Don't worry, your mother has it all sorted out. You two just enjoy being guests."

He walks away and Patrick spins me around and kisses me.

"Hey! No fair!" I exclaim and he grabs me and wraps his arm around me.

"I don't care about morning breath, I don't care if you're sick, I don't care what you wear. Elizabeth Riley, you are the most beautiful woman I have ever met. I have waited six months to kiss you, and I'm not going to let something so superficial get in the way. Trust me, you are worth the six months, you are worth a lifetime of waiting. But now that I have you, I'm not letting you go."

He pulls me in by the waist and kisses me again. My heart feels as if it wants to escape out of my chest. I pull away and look into his eyes, "Who knew that you're such a romantic?"

"Well maybe if you hadn't friend zoned me you would have found out sooner." He winks at me.

My jaw drops open, "Hey! I didn't- okay fine." I huff. I stand on my tiptoes and kiss him on the cheek. "I'm going to take a shower. See you in a bit."

I twirl around and grab everything out of my suitcase that I need. I take time alone to replay the events of the past several weeks: Patrick asking me to the wedding, how our daily lives have shifted, and that kiss. I feel lighter just thinking about it. I start humming in the shower, I don't remember the last time I felt so relaxed. All of a sudden, it hits me- I haven't thought of the nightmare. In fact, I didn't have it for a second time.

The shampoo bottle I'm holding clangs to the bottom of the tub. Are things finally over? Has Patrick been the key all along? I've spent the past six months fighting the past, only to realize that everything I have been hopelessly praying for was just in front of me? Am I really that stupid.

I hurry and finish my shower, wanting to make up for all the lost time. I get dressed and wrap my hair in a towel. I walk to the dining room and am greeted by Patrick's whole family. It seems kind of intimidating at first, they are all smiling at me. Patrick's got his mother's smile but his father's sense of humor. I love how cozy their home is, it's a house filled with love.

"Good mornin' sweetheart!" His mom exclaims. "I made pancakes and sausage. I'm sure it won't be as good as the cinnamon rolls Patrick says you make-

"Mom!"

"Oh hush. If you didn't want us to tell her anything you shouldn't have told us." His mom states.

I sit down and reach under the table for Patrick's hand, I give it a squeeze. "Well, I would just love to hear what all he has told you."

He rolls his eyes, but the embarrassment spreads across his cheeks.

"Well, he definitely undersold how beautiful you are; so you can discuss that later. He also goes on and on. About you whenever we call. I mean, he left early after Christmas because he wanted to be with you. I have never seen him so-"

"MOM!"

I can't help but laugh, Patrick is covering his face with his hand. "I guess I must be popular then."

"Oh, you are, but you know, he hasn't been in a relationship since the beginning of college. And we never met her, so it's nice to finally have a girl over."

"Mom we aren't in a-"

"Oh hush, both of you have been holding hands under the table since she sat down." His mom states before taking a bite of her bacon.

This time it's my turn to blush, but Patrick squeezes my hand. I feel suddenly bashful and take a bite out of the pancakes.

"Also, Patrick made me get the centerpiece for you." She nods at the flowers on the table.

"Daisies!" I gasp.

"Well, there goes any chance of being nonchalant."

Both me and his mom laugh.

His dad places down his mug and shakes his head. "As soon as you said Elizabeth was coming, you should have known this would happen. Now, I'm going to get to the store so someone can make a cake later." He winks at me. "Suzanne, let's go."

His mother gets up and takes their plates away, finally I'm left alone with Patrick. And I suddenly realize I still have a towel on my head. "I must look like a sight here."

"You look beautiful."

I feel the corner of my lip upturn, "So, they think we are in a relationship."

"It would seem that way."

I nod and look at my plate. "Do you think we could....take it slow? I mean, all we have done is kissed. And there are things...things I'm not ready to talk about yet. I just need time." I look down at my plate. "Trust me, I am so ready for this change, but I don't want to be..."

Patrick tilts my chin up and I slowly meet his gaze. "I want you to be able to take your time. I know you have been through a lot. You call the shots here, as long as I can be with you. That's all I want.

I smile and lean over and kiss him. "I don't deserve you." I whisper.

⁕⁕⁕

Patrick spent the day showing me around the town. He showed me where he went to school, then places he hung out such as the movie theater, and the skating rink. We went to a BBQ restaurant so that I could have brisket the Texas way. And now we are taking a walk in the park.

"I think I enjoy the fact we aren't fighting hills for tonight's walk." I giggle.

Patrick nods, "If there is one thing I don't miss, it's the steep hill at the end of your street. I didn't want to admit it after our first walk, but I was about out of breath! You have kept me in shape though; I would have gained quite a few pounds from all those cinnamon cakes if we didn't go on walks."

I laugh and loop my arm through his, "Speaking of which, how much do you talk about me to your parents?"

He nodded. "Oh...whenever mom calls each week. She asks about you- I don't bring- Yeah, but you don't have to make the cake." He changes the subject, "He may never let you leave."

We sit on a bench, and he rests his arm around me.

"So, tell me about this friend who's getting married tomor-row."

"Her name is Regan. She was part of my high school friend group. Most of the group still hangs out, some have even gotten married." He shrugs. "Of course, when I left for Tennessee in college I stopped seeing her as much. I'm excited for you to meet them all tomorrow."

I smile back at him, "I'm excited to meet them too.

# Chapter Seventeen

## PATRICK

After we get back to my parents' we decide to lounge in the house and appreciate a day off. We sit on the couch, and I instantly pull Elizabeth into me as soon as she sits next to me. She giggles as she lays her head on my chest.

I hand her the remote and she scrolls until she settles for *The Office*. "This is heaven, my favorite show and my favorite guy. I'm so happy."

I kiss the top of her head. "Me too. So, I have a question?"

"Hmm?" She leans back to look up at me.

"Can I take you on a date tonight?"

"Tonight? Why not when we get back?" She moves to the side to look better at me.

"Because I've waited six months to ask you that question. And I don't want to wait another night to take you out."

She kisses me on the cheek, "I would love to go on a date tonight. Where are we going?"

I pull her back to me and look at the TV, "A nice restaurant, similar to last night. But tonight, we are ditching my parents."

She chuckles and I feel her shift her weight onto me, I hug her tighter as we fall into silence watching the TV. I mindlessly rub her arm and play with her hair, I honestly haven't been paying attention to the show, just to the woman in my arms.

After a couple of episodes, she sits up and stretches. "Well, I need to go get ready, I have a date with an incredibly handsome guy tonight." She winks.

"Oh, yeah? Tell me about him."

She leans in closer to me. "Oh, he is nothing short of a hero. He is always there when I need him; he even saved a kid from crashing on his scooter once. But he is sweet, charming, and a good listener. And I have been incredibly lucky to have him in my life."

"He sounds like the lucky one, I've been trying to date you for months and haven't had a chance."

She laughs and kisses me. "Okay goober, I'll see you in a little bit.

I watch her walk away, feeling lighter than before. I head into the kitchen to do some dishes to help my mom out while I kill some time before I need to get ready. Once I have finished cleaning up, I head into my room, taking a look around. This is the first time I've seen this room as a thing from my past. My old track medals are still hanging on the wall, and old vinyl that I listened to in high school. Back then I always dreamed about the future and what it holds, for once I don't wish for the future anymore. I'm happy with what I have now.

I put on a dark green button-up and some khakis. I go into the bathroom and comb my hair up, making sure it sits right. When I walk out, Elizabeth is leaning against the wall wearing a pink dress and her hair is pinned back.

"Wow." I whisper.

"What?" She gives her dress a small twist.

"You are stunning, I can't believe I get to take you out tonight."

She grins and strides over to kiss me. "I'm the one in disbelief." She whispers.

I grab her hand and escort her out to my dad's car, holding the door open for her. Once I get in, she reaches over for my hand. I can't help but smile at her and reach over to rest my hand on her lap.

"I haven't been on a date in so long, I'm not sure what to talk about." I chuckle.

She shakes her head, "Well neither do I. I guess...tell me about your biggest fear."

"Wow, getting deep before dinner. Okay...um. Well, I would say I'm afraid of failure. I was a top student in school and a star track runner. That's why I focused on work in college up to now and moved out to help with owning our whole business."

I see her nodding in the corner of my eye, and she squeezes my hand. "You've really done quite well for yourself."

I nod, I know I'm going to ask for conversation-sake but I'm nervous. "What about you?"She sighs, "I'm scared of being alone. Not in the relationship way, but in the dying alone way. I always want people to feel loved, but it's also because I want to feel loved. That old saying about putting out what you want to receive in life is something I live by. I'm terrified of people turning against me.

I pull her hand up to my lips. "Elizabeth, you don't need to worry about that at all. I have dealt with your town and how people want to protect you. You are far from dying alone and being turned against."

I glance at her, and she gives me a shy smile. "Well, this is it." I say as we turn into the parking lot. I decided to take her to a nice Italian restaurant. I hold her hand on the way in and wait for us to be seated. She shifts on her feet until she steps closer to me, I put my hand on her lower back, which earns me a smile.

Once we get seated, she smirks at me. "So, I have a question that I've been dying to ask you."

I raise a brow at her, "And what's that?"

"Well. I've been wondering about when you realized you had feelings for me?"

I feel my cheeks turn bright red and I smile, "Well...when do you think I got feelings for you?"

She takes a piece of the bread that was placed on our table and tears a piece of it off. "I think you feel for me the day you came to help me at the bakery."

I smile thinking of that day, but I shake my head as she pops the piece of bread into her mouth. "That was a good day, but not quite."

She raises her eyebrows, "After?" I shake my head. She taps on her chin trying to think. Her eyes widen with realization, "On the day we met?"

I smile and nod, "Is that weird, I'm sorry if that's weird."

"No no, I just thought- Katie was right." She laughs. "What happened that night to ignite these feelings?"

"Well, you happened. You opened the door and welcomed me with open arms. I have never met someone that's so kind and loving to anybody. That night I already felt at home, and I had only been in town for the thirty-minute drive. You brought light into what was a really bad day." I reach across the table and grab her hand. "Thank you for welcoming me that night."

This time it's her turn to blush and she squeezes my hand back. "Of course, I'm glad I did. Well, you will never guess when I realized I had feelings for you."

"You're right." I laugh, "I definitely won't." I run my thumb over her fingers.

"I guess it started when you came to help me at the bakery. Like you planted a seed that day that I refused to water. But you watered it each time you would show up for me or others, like when you stopped Carson from crashing. And you are always showing up for me. You are the person I call when something is wrong. I was going to tell you that I had feelings for you the night that you showed up with Becca...but you showed up with Becca."

She purses her lips, "And I got extremely jealous. That's why I didn't talk with you for a while because I thought I had taken too long and lost my chance."

I squeeze her hand but don't get the chance to say anything as it's our chance to order. When the waiter takes our menus away, I reach across the table and grab both of her hands. "Elizabeth, I have long since made the decision that I want you in my life. You will never lose your chance to be with me, and it looks like you never have to find out. Here we are, on our first of many dates."

We continue to talk about life, getting to know each other now on this different level. While we are talking, I notice her eyes keep glancing over at the dessert placard on the table.

"Do you want to get dessert?"

"Oh no, we don't have-"

"Get whatever you want, I want you to leave tonight hoping to get a second date with me." I say with a wink.

She bursts with a laugh and leans towards me, "What makes you think you're getting a second date?"

"Maybe because your eyes keep falling to my lips all night."

"Well, that's because you have some sauce on them."

I quickly grab a napkin, "Do I really? Why didn't you-" I wipe my mouth quickly and it comes off clean. "You little liar."

She claps her hands together and leans forward, "That was just too easy. Maybe I was staring at your lips because I can't wait to kiss you, but we are in public, and I don't like PDA."

I lean forward as well, "I feel the exact same."

We are interrupted by our waiter, and I order the dessert she's been eyeing, which wins me a grateful smile.

After we finish dessert and I pay, we are walking back to the car hand-in-hand, when she turns to me and places her hand on my cheek and pulls me down. The kiss is gentle, but it lingers. She starts to pull away, and I pull her back in for another.

When we pull apart, I linger near her. "I thought you don't like PDA?"

"That was before I realized how much I love kissing you." She smiles and gives me a quick peck before turning back to the car.

When we arrive at my parents' I start to walk her to the door when I stop, pulling her with a jolt toward me. "So, on a normal date, we would just say goodnight and end the night here. But instead, we are going inside together." I grasp both of her hands and pull them to my chest. "And my parents are in there."

Her eyes shine at me, "So what are you saying?"

"Well, I want to ask you a question. Give you a goodnight kiss, and then both of us get cozy on the couch before going off to bed."

"That sounds wonderful, what's your question?"

"Did you enjoy our date?"

"That was the best first date I've ever been on." She smiles.

"So that's a yes to a second date?"

She pulls my arms around her and leans into my chest, standing on her tiptoes and kisses me. My arms wrap tighter around her as I kiss her, deepening the kiss for just a moment. She pulls her face from mine and smiles at me. "That's a yes to many more dates."

I grin at her and take her hand to bring her back inside. We both get changed into comfier clothes and meet each other on the couch. I turn on the TV and leave the channel on whatever my dad last had on.

Elizabeth plops down next to me, her hair is now in a messy bun, and she is sporting leggings and my hoodie.

I put my arm around her and lean into her. "Did I ever tell you how much I love seeing you in my hoodie?"

She smirks at me and shakes her head. "I do recall you saying that I can keep it though."

I kiss her cheek and pull her down on me, so that I can lie on the couch. She curls herself into me. And I start to rub her back. "You can have all of my hoodies if that's what you want."

She nods and we fall into comfortable silence as we watch TV. It doesn't take long, but I feel her weight sink into me and her breathing deepens.  I decided to wait until the end of the movie to carry her to bed. I grab the remote and turn the volume down, not wanting anything to wake her up.

I easily pick her up and carry her to her room. When I lay her down she lets out a soft groan and grabs my arm. "Don't go." She murmurs.

"I'll be just across the hall." I reply softly.

"Please, just until I fall asleep." I brush a piece of hair out of her face and kiss her cheek. I really don't want to leave her so I crawl into bed next to her.

She wraps herself in my arms and curls into my chest. I feel her plant a kiss on my shoulder, and she closes her eyes. "Goodnight Patty." She whispers.

"Goodnight." I say back and run my fingers through her hair and gently on her back.  I rub her back until her breathing shifts.

"I love you." I whisper.

# Chapter Eighteen



### PATRICK

The morning of the wedding, I'm lounging on the couch with my dad. The smell of hairspray fills the house as the women are getting ready. Thirty minutes before we need to leave, I hear my mom rustle into the room.

"What are you two doing?! We've got to go!" She shoos us off the couch and I amble to my room. It really doesn't take me long to get ready, so I walk back to the couch after I get dressed and style my hair over. I hear heels tap their way closer, I look up from my phone to see Elizabeth, coming to me as if out of a dream. Her hair is curled and cascading down her shoulders, that green dress makes her blue eyes shine.

"What?" She says when she sees me staring.

"You are a vision."

She blushes and tucks back a strand of hair. "Thanks. You clean up nice yourself. Is everyone ready."

I nod towards my parents' room. "They should be done any minute now." I stand and close the distance between us, wrapping my arms around her.

My parents emerge from their room right as I'm about to kiss her. "Okay, let's go! Don't want to be late!" I let out a small groan and Elizabeth smirks at me, giving my arm a squeeze.

Once we sit in the car, she reaches for my hand and weaves our fingers together. Her thumb starts mindlessly drawing circles on the back of my hand. I keep stealing glances at her, every time we catch each other looking we both smile.

As we pull up to the venue, I see that it's a beautiful building that is almost completely made out of glass, it must make the most heavenly lighting. We walk in and see signs everywhere that range from: 'Husband & Wife', 'Mr. & Mrs.', 'T', 'Mr. & Mrs. Taylor'. I put my arm around Elizabeth and guide her to find some seats, my parents trailing behind us.

"Pat!" I hear and turn to see an old high school friend, Bryan.

"Bryan! Nice to see you." I give him a hug and then extend my arm towards Elizabeth. "This is Elizabeth, did you bring Claire?" He reaches his hand to Elizabeth to shake hers.

"No, she couldn't make it. Wow, it looks like Pat finally found someone. Elizabeth, is he treating you right?"

She giggles and nods, "Patty is very good to me." She leans in closer to me and grabs my hand. I look down and I notice something is off in her eyes. She looks uncomfortable for some reason. I end the small talk with Bryan and continue walking to get us seats. I see my parents have gone ahead to sit down, so I guide her to join them. I put my arm around her, and other people are coming by to catch up as they come into the room.

"Look, it's the Williams family!" I turn and see my friends Dana and Mike walking up to us.

"Well look who we have here!" My dad laughs and gets up to greet them. Dana is another family friend, my parents have known hers for twenty years.

Dana makes eye contact with me then her eyes glide to Elizabeth. "Mike, Pat has a date!" Mike looks over quickly. "Look at her! Way to go Pat!" I suddenly feel self-conscious; if Elizabeth is already feeling uncomfortable, I don't want more attention drawn to her. I change the topic to Dana's job as a teacher, she usually talks about that for a while. My parents jump into the conversation, and I look back at Elizabeth who is looking sadly around the room. I reach over and grab her hand; she looks up at me, and I give her a small squeeze to let her know I got her. She stares at me for a long second and then looks back at my friends.

"One of my best friends is a teacher," Elizabeth pipped in. "I always look forward to the stories she tells. I have so much respect for what you do." She smiles at Dana, who grins back.

"Well thank you. So how do you know Pat?"

She looks at me, and a corner of her lip rises, "He lived a couple houses down from me and we became fast friends." Her eyes stay on me as she speaks, and I feel my face instantly warm. She squeezes my hand before turning back to Dana. She motions to her dress, "I'm assuming you're a bridesmaid?"

Dana nods and continues telling Elizabeth about how the group of us all grew up in high school together. Elizabeth starts to relax, and I let go of her hand to put it on the small of her back. Mike comes over after a few minutes catching up with my dad and takes Dana to get ready for the ceremony.

I sit down and Elizabeth follows suit, out of the corner of my eye, I notice she picks up the wedding program. Suddenly,

I feel her body completely tense up again next to me, I look at her, and she is completely pale. "Eliza-"

"I'll be right back." She stands and rushes out of the room.

# Chapter Nineteen



I run into the bathroom to compose myself, I can't believe this is happening. This would be my luck. I let myself have the opportunity for love, and the universe decides to throw a curveball right back at me. I walk out of the bathroom and keep my eyes to the ground, I don't want anyone looking at me or recognizing me. I clearly am not coordinated enough to do this because I ran smack into someone's back.

"Oh, I'm so sorry, I-" Oh no, it's *him*. I feel the tears well up in my eyes.

"Elizabeth?" Blake questions, the shock of his face quickly turning to anger. "What are you doing here?"

"I didn't know. I'm sorry. I didn't want this to happen. I-"

"Seriously, what the hell is wrong with you? You cheat on me and then you have the nerve to show up on my wedding day?"

"No, I-"

"You know what, everyone was right. They all talked about how you were too good to do that to me, and that there must be something more to the story. But here you are, showing up again to ruin my life. What did you think? Do you need to ruin my life just a little more? Cause you won't, I refuse."

I feel short of breath and tears trickle down my cheeks. "Blake please."

"No, Elizabeth. I need answers. Why are you here?"

All of a sudden, I feel a hand on the small of my back. I look to see Patrick at my side. A battle tugs in me, relief that he is by my side, but anxiety of him now being thrown into this mess.

"Is everything okay over here?" Patrick asks. Blake's eyes looked down, and he saw his arm around me.

"Oh, so is this him? Is this him? Wow Elizabeth, I can't believe it." He scoffs, his behavior draws attention, and I see his parents walking over behind him. He's going to start pacing; he paces when he's upset. On cue, he takes three steps and turns around to repeat.

I turn towards Patrick. "We need to go."

"Elizabeth! What the hell are you doing here? Haven't you done enough to hurt my son?!" His mom exclaimed.

I open my mouth to speak but Patrick steps in. "Woah, everyone calm down. I invited her to the wedding. Now will someone please explain to me what is going on?"

Blake looks at me dead in the eye, I can see all the hurt and anger in his eyes. Just like the day I ended our engagement. "Elizabeth, how about you explain this?"

I stare at Blake and then my eyes dart around the room, seeing all the people we knew staring at me and starting to whisper to each other. "Please, Blake. Please, don't." My voice cracks and turns into a whisper.

"She cheated on me." He blurts, his eyes still locked on mine, I feel the daggers of his words stabbing my heart. "Two months before our wedding."

I look down, not wanting to look into Patrick's eyes or see his shame. I can already feel enough coming from the three people in front of me.

"Come on sweetie, we need you to cool down before you walk down the aisle." Blake's mom says, her voice softer as she tries to soothe him as they turn to leave. I keep my eyes to the ground. I hear a lot of movement around me as the next thirty seconds lasts a lifetime. All the whispers, all the gossip.

"Hey, are you okay?" *Patrick.*

"I-I'm fine." My voice is shaky, "Can I please leave now?" I whisper, I force myself to look up at him. His eyes don't hold the shame I expect them to, but worry.

"Of course. Let's go." He starts to reach for me but I flinch away.

I spin on my heels back to look at Patrick. "No, I will go. These are your friends, stay." I turn back around and rush to the exit, not wanting to argue with him.

I just want to be out. Out of this building, out of this state. I need to be home. I can feel Patrick close behind me, but I'm not in the mood to push anymore. He gets an Uber and wraps his arm around me, his stability makes me realize that I'm shaking. I tuck my face into his neck. "Why did you make me come?" I cry out, he continues to hold me until the driver arrives and takes us to the house.

"Did you know?" I whisper.

# Chapter Twenty

### PATRICK

I open the door to the house for Elizabeth, but her eyes stay on the floor. She walks into her room and closes the door shut.

"Elizabeth!"

"Oh my gosh, Patrick. Just leave me alone!" I can tell she's crying again, she held it together most of the ride here.

"Just tell me what is going on!" I had only heard parts of the conversation before I had approached, but he said she cheated on him. That couldn't be true...could it? "Please, Lizzy, just talk to me."

She opens the door, her face is stained from her mascara. What were perfect curls this morning was now sloppily put up in a bun, most of it falling out around her face.

"You didn't answer me earlier, did you know?! Did you know this was Blake's wedding and you brought me anyways??"

I take a step back, "No…I had no idea it was his wedding. I've never met him…I wouldn't have even come if I had known." I grab both of her hands in mine. "I definitely wouldn't have invited you if I had known, I would *never* do that to you."

She stares at me for a second and I can tell she doesn't know what to say, she lets go of my hands and closes the door once more and so I knock on it again. "Lizzy please. Talk to me."

She swings the door open quickly. "What? You heard what he said, I cheated. It's all out in the open now. So go ahead and judge me." She swung the door to close it, but I stuck my hand out to catch it. She looks at me with wide eyes and storms past me. She stomps into the kitchen and starts throwing open cabinets. She finds what she is looking for, or close to it, my dad's whiskey. She pours a finger of it and chugs it. She glares back at me, with a challenge in her eyes wanting me to bring up what we fought about earlier this year. But despite that I can see all the pain and brokenness in her eyes.

"I'm not judging you." I say softly.

She rolls her eyes, "Oh come on. We both know how you feel about me. Now you are wondering if I would do the same to you."

I shake my head and step towards her, but she backs away.

"I promise, I'm not thinking that." I frown.

Tears glide down her cheeks, "I should've never let you kiss me."

I feel taken aback by her words. I sit down on the arm of the couch. Seeing how she is acting, I won't win by protesting against her, she wants to hurt me.

She leans up against the wall and sinks to the floor, clutching the empty glass to her chest. After a few minutes she starts to take a few deep breaths.

"Elizabeth, please talk to me." I lean forward, resting my elbows on my knees. "I know you. And I just think there may be more to the story. Tell me your side." She avoids looking at me and keeps shaking her head.

"Please."

Her eyes shoot to mine, "How do you know?"

"How do I know what?" I wonder.

She lets out a puff of air, "How do you know there is more to the story? That I didn't cheat?"

"Because someone who cheated and didn't care about their ex wouldn't hold on to their picture. They wouldn't have a complete come apart seeing it three years later. They wouldn't refuse love for three years. They wouldn't have as much hurt in their eyes from seeing them. They wouldn't act like this" I motion to her. "You didn't cheat. I just can't figure out why you hate yourself so much."

The tears drip from her face onto her chest, "I hurt him."

"What....what do you mean?"

She begins weeping and I instinctively get on the floor next to her and put my arms around her. She pushes me away, so I place my hands in my lap.

"I really hurt him." I frown at her, but she won't look at me, "If I tell you, you won't see me the same way."

I shake my head, "Not possible."

Her lip trembles and looks down at her fingers. "I-I..."

I take a deep breath reaching over and grabbing her hand, hoping she won't turn away this time. "If you are absolutely not ready to talk, you don't have to. But after tonight....I think you need to talk to someone."

"No, I need to do this. You're right" Her voice cracks and she quickly looks up at me. "Blake was it. He was the one, the love of my life." I feel a sting in my heart, but I keep looking at her. She is avoiding eye contact, her eyes are searching the floor. "And I ruined it. And now...he's really gone." She looks up at me, her eyes fill with crocodile tears. "I lied. I knew things wouldn't be the same. He would see me differently just like you will. And I lied because it is easier than the truth."

I look at her confused and shake my head. "I'm not going to see you differently. I promise. Just...trust me. *Please*."

She nods slightly and I feel her hand start shaking in mine. "Just a couple of months before the wedding, I had a long day at work, and all the stress of the wedding was really getting to me. So, I went to the bar just for a drink or two. I really never drank that much but I just needed some sort of relief."

She pauses for a second, still staring down at our hands. "There was this guy at the bar, he was friendly and was letting me vent about my day and all the stress I was under. After I finished my drink, I started to head out to my car, but I realized I was a bit under the influence. I was terribly light weight back then, but this wasn't normal. I started to turn back into the bar to get some water to sober up, but-the guy- he grabbed my arm."

Elizabeth starts to get out of breath. I was able to piece together what happened next. I put my arm around her and pull her to my chest. She begins sobbing again and I feel so many emotions. Heartbreak for her, hatred for the guy that did this to her, and the desire to fix it all.

"Elizabeth, I'm so, so sorry. You didn't deserve that. You are so strong for being who you are now." All that I think I can do is just sit here and hold her. After a few moments I pull back and wipe the tears off her face.

"So, why did you tell him you cheated? He would have understood."

She started shaking her head, "No...he wouldn't. Just like your idea of me just changed, his would have too. So it was easier to lie."

I held her face in my hands, forcing her to look at me. "Hey, listen to me. I do *not* see you differently. What happened to you isn't your fault. You are hurt, but who I know now, this girl in front of me. She is resilient, she is strong, and she is *good*. She may be broken but she is pushing through. You are so much more than this. *Do not* belittle yourself because a horrible person tried to belittle you."

She starts crying again and lays her head on my chest, so I wrap my arms tightly around her. "When you had to come pick me up from work." She starts quietly, "I thought I saw him outside."

I freeze at the realization. I had almost forgotten the day she had a breakdown at work. It all made sense now, I squeeze her as close as I can. I know there's nothing I can do right now to help.

"I'm so sorry, Elizabeth."

When her cries soften and her shaking resides. She sits up and looks at me for a long second before placing her hand on my cheek. "Patty, you are so wonderful. I don't deserve you."

I reach up and put my hand over hers. "You deserve everything. You are the only one who doesn't see how wonderful you are. You are loved and cherished, and I will tell you that every day until you finally believe it."

I let go of her and reach up to wipe her face with my thumbs. I keep hold of her face, forcing her to look at me again. "You are the sweetest, most wonderful person. I knew that from the first minute I met you. Everyone adores you, your entire essence is love. Don't talk to me about doing better. Even though he is it for you, you are *it* for me."

She shakes her head and whimpers. "I'm not ready."

"That's okay, you can take your time."

"No, you don't get it. It's been three years and I'm not ready." She starts playing with her fingers and I let my hands fall back to my lap. "You are the first person I have felt safe with, but

I can only…I'm not going to be what you want. I may never be able to fully trust a guy." She looks at me with tear filled eyes. "I have to let you go."

My heart plummets and twists. "No, Elizabeth. No. Don't push me away."

"I have to Patty. Don't you see it? I'm never going to be what you want me to be. I am completely broken. I may never trust you and be the girl you want me to be. You deserve better."

"*Stop* saying that." I protest. "I fell in love with *you*. The girl whose house I accidentally showed up at and I kept showing up at for the following six months. The girl who spends all her days wanting to provide the best for her customers, family, and friends. I have always known you were broken, but all I want to do is help glue the pieces back together. So please, let me do that."

She looks up at me with her teary eyes, her eyes searching mine. "You love me?"

I grab her hand and hold it on my chest. "I do and I fall in love with you more every day. *Nothing* you have said today changes that. You can't change it. My heart only wants you."

Her lip quivers and she reaches up and strokes my hair. I stare down into her eyes, she leans up and kisses my cheek. I smile softly, at her and I reach over to wipe some more tears off her face.

"You are too kind to me. I-" I place my thumb against her lip.

"Don't you dare say you don't deserve me. I have already told you how amazing you are. *You* are the only person who needs to accept this. No one else. You got it?"

She nods and uses her arm to wipe her face. I stand then pick her up, carrying her to the couch. "Stay there."

I head into the bathroom and wet a hand towel, I come back into the room, sitting next to her I begin wiping all the smeared makeup from her face. When I finish, she takes the towel from my hand and places it on the coffee table. She leans forward and kisses me, but this wasn't like any we have shared before. This was a passionate kiss, a *needing* kiss. She wraps her arms around my neck, and I pull her to my lap. Our lips never parted from each other. I keep holding her close until I feel her hands at my waist and she starts to unbutton my shirt. I sit back and push her hands away. "No."

"What?"

"I said no."

"I'm just trying to give you what you want."

I shake my head. "If you think all I want is your body you are very wrong. Elizabeth, you are very emotional. I'm not going to take advantage of you. I shouldn't have even kissed you just now, since you were just trying to push me away five minutes ago. And I agree you need to take things slow."

Her eyes stare at me in disbelief, so I take her hand in mine. "I want you, yes. But not tonight, in fact not even until we are married. So that can wait a long time."

"You...marriage."

I smile at her and squeeze her hand. "One day, yes, but let's get there first." I stand and pull her up. "Let's get you to bed. You've had a day."

I lead her to her room and stand at the door. "Goodnight Elizabeth, sweet dreams." As I walk back to my room, I realize something. Her nightmares: it must be of that night. My heart breaks a little more, knowing she has had to relive that almost every day.

I feel myself drifting to sleep when I hear someone open my door. I sit up and Elizabeth comes tiptoeing in my room. She crawls into the bed next to me.

"I'm not going to do anything...I just don't want to be alone." She stares at me, her eyes sparkling from the tears still in them. I lean over and kiss her forehead and put an arm around her.

"You don't need to feel alone anymore."

# Chapter Twenty-One



At four in the morning, I get up and frown at Patrick sleeping peacefully next to me. I didn't really sleep through the night, the events of the day play on repeat in my mind. He looks so content and perfect. I tiptoe back to my room and start packing up my things. When I finish, I find a piece of scratch paper and take a pen out of my purse.

*Patrick,*

*I'm so sorry for doing this. But you deserve so much more. I've gone home, but you need to stay and enjoy this time in Texas. I'm sorry to have ruined your trip. I won't contact you anymore, I* have already caused too much pain, and I'm sorry to keep playing games with you. Thank you for always being there for me.

Elizabeth

I sneak into his room, I hold back my tears and place the note on his nightstand. I had ordered an Uber when I first went into my room. I see that it's approaching now so I head outside. As soon as I get in the car, I book the redeye to Nashville. I feel my world is crashing down on me, how much longer can I continue on like this?

# Chapter Twenty-Two

## PATRICK

I wake up and it takes me a minute to become fully co-herent before the past 24 hours come back to my mind. I glance at the clock, 8:04. I roll over and something is amiss. Elizabeth isn't there, I get up to head to her room.

"Elizabeth?" I call out, silence. There is no one in the bathroom or the kitchen. I run back to my room to grab my phone when I see the note by it. I feel a punch to my gut as I read it, slowly sitting down.

"Why does she have to push people away?" I whisper.

I get up and start packing my things, I'm not staying here. She needs to see that she can't push people away because it's an easy thing to do. She needs to see that she is so much more than what happened to her. I went ahead and ordered an Uber so that it would arrive by the time I'm done packing. I know she is probably in the air, it could have been hours ago that she left.

8:23

Elizabeth, where are you?

8:30

You can't push me away, YOU deserve better. You need to see you are worth fighting for. I'm not going to let you go.

8:30

Are you okay?

The Uber finally arrives and I head down, staring out the window.

8:40

Elizabeth please don't end this. Stop running.

I decide to put my phone away, but my heart leaps when it starts to vibrate. I look down but it's just my mom calling. Disappointment starts to set in.

"Hello?"

"Pat? What happened yesterday?? Where are you?" Her voice is full of concern.

"It's a long story...but I'm headed to the airport." I feel my voice break. I look out the window, after a few seconds I manage to muster: "She's gone, mom."

"Well then you need to go and get her." My mom says.

"That's what I'm doing, that's why I'm leaving. I'm sorry and tell everyone I'm sorry." I hang up, not wanting to get into this with my mom. My leg bounces up and down, I restrain the urge to keep looking at the time. I was able to get a flight that takes off in two hours, and I'm praying that she is on the same flight as me.

As soon as I make it through security, I run to the gate without putting my shoes back on. She isn't here, she's already gone.

My leg continues to bounce as I wait for the flight to board. Eventually I stand up and pace back and forth. I need to move, to get out of here. I feel some eyes on me, I realize how crazy I must look so I sit back down.

I need to save this relationship, no, this friendship, I can take whatever she has to offer right now. Sure, I screwed up, we shouldn't have made out last night. But she will see that we are stronger than this, right?

When my boarding group is called and I board the plane, I'm just a couple hours from being with Elizabeth and making things right. I want to try to work on some paperwork on the plane ride like I did before. But as soon as I start to read a document, everything blurs as I try to think of some other way to show her how *good* she is. The moments tick by, I close my eyes and pray. I pray for the right words, for her heart to soften, for her to receive healing. I also pray for patience and understanding. I want to be able to be there for her but what she is dealing with is so much. And I know I don't have all the answers except: she deserves love.

The second the plane jolts from landing, I turn my phone off airplane mode. Not a single text.

I take an Uber straight to her house. I click on her name dozens of times on the thirty-minute ride over. I type, I delete, I type again, I toss my phone to the side. When we pull into her neighborhood, it takes all my restraint to not tell my driver to speed up. My hand rests on the door handle and the second he comes to a stop, I jump out. I run up to her door and look around frantically. Where does she keep her spare key? I know she told me it was somewhere...the pot! I dig into the dirt and pull out the spare key. As I open the door, I hear glass shattering and then a cry.

"Elizabeth!" I run into the house.

"Seriously, Patrick? Why can't you just go away. Just leave me alone!" She yells, her voice hoarse.

"If you can be a hundred percent honest with me that you want to be alone then yes. But I don't believe you. I see-"

I round the corner into the kitchen, there's a broken wine glass on the floor. Elizabeth is standing next to it, facing the counter. Another wine glass in her hand and a bottle in the other. Tears run down her face, I notice blood on her hand. I step forward and grab her wrist, she tries to jerk back but I tighten my grip, I take the new glass from her hand and set it down, I bring her hand under the sink and run water over it. There is a small gash at the bottom of her palm.

I feel her eyes on me, I loosen my grip on her wrist and search a nearby drawer for a bandage. I let go of her and take the adhesive out of the packaging; as I tend her wound, she begins violently shaking. I wrap my other arm around her, and she turns into me, putting her forehead on my chest as she gives out. I quickly catch her, and lower myself to the floor, letting her collapse into me. She begins wailing, and I soothe her once more, rubbing her back as her tears soak into my shirt.

I look around the kitchen and notice an empty bottle sticking out of the trash can and the wine on the floor from the broken wine glass. She needs to get away from her temptation, I move my arms around her body and pick her up to carry her to the couch. When I sit, she clings to me, needing to be held.

It takes several minutes but she is finally calming down, "Y-you sh-should g-go." But she curls more into me.

"Is that what you want?"

She shakes her head into my chest and then pulls her head to look at me. Her eyes bare into mine, searching for answers then slowly down to my lips, her thumb runs over my lips. She frowns at me and tucks her head under my chin. I am desperate to know what she is thinking, but I have a feeling I don't want to know.

As I held her, time paused. The only sound is her sniffling every few minutes. I feel my leg falling asleep when she looks at me once more and then pulls away. I slide her off of me, knowing she must be dehydrated if she has been crying all morning- and all of last night.

"Pat-no." She is leaning to get up, reaching for me with desperate eyes.

I turn back quickly, "Just one moment." I reach for her hand and give it a squeeze. "I'll be right back."

I step over the broken glass and quickly fill a cup and come back to her.

I hand her the water, which she eagerly takes "Thanks." Her lips are already on the rim. When she finished drinking, I took the glass from her and put it on the table. I take both of her hands in mine.

"Elizabeth Riley, over the past few months I have seen how you have handled the last time you pushed someone away. You know you wish you never did that, and I don't want you to push me away and have the same reaction." She whimpers and uses the arm of her sweater to wipe her face.

"But *I'm* not going to let you push me away. It's time you finally stopped running, it will only bring you more pain."

She picks a string off the hem of her sweater. "I shouldn't have run. You didn't deserve that." Her blue eyes slowly meet mine. "But you need to understand-"

"Don't you dare say that any of this is unfixable. And that you deserve to hurt, because you don't."

"But Patr-"

"No Elizabeth. I moved to this town and *everyone* talked about how you are practically untouchable. Even your best friends don't know what you are going through. Stop making people live on your terms. All these people love you. And they want to help you. Stop pushing everyone away. *It's not your fault.*"

Her defiant eyes lock on mine and eventually they soften. "You're right." She sighs and starts playing with the string again. "I don't think I can tell them though."

"You don't need to tell them right now. But you need to talk to *someone.* There are licensed people who can help."

She slowly nods and her teary eyes look up at mine. "We can't be together though...I can't...I'm not-I'm not ready."

I lean forward and kiss her forehead.

"I know, it's okay. I'm going to be here through this with you, though. I'm not going anywhere." I pull her into my chest. "You're my best friend above everything else."

I hold her, being what she needs for right now until I feel her weight fall onto me. I carry her to her bedroom. After I get her between the blankets, I head to the kitchen. I clean up the broken glass and spilled wine. I fill another glass of water and place it with some aspirin on her bedside table.

I grab a pen and paper.

*Call me when you need me. I'll be here in thirty. You won't be alone in this again.*

# Chapter Twenty-Three

*Elizabeth*

It's only been a week since we got back from Texas, and now that I have been forced to face my reality, I can't keep my emotions at bay anymore. Each night when I came home this week, I would start with two glasses of wine instead of my usual one. If Patrick knew he would probably start driving me home. He has gotten overprotective with me since we got back. He has been incredibly consistent with coming over every night, but I can't let this continue on anymore.

I can see how much it is killing him that we can't be together romantically. And I have been selfish enough to continue taking his time, which I know is creating hope for him that he can be with me one day. I pick up my phone and book an appointment with a therapist and then call Patrick.

He answers after one ring. "Hey, is everything okay at work?"

"Yeah, um." I take a deep breath. "Just listen to everything I have to say, okay?"

"Oh-uh-okay?" He sounds nervous.

"We can't hang out tonight. Go and take some time for yourself. I am sending you some money for anything, just because of all you have done for me in the past…six months, especially this past week…I-I'm going to therapy, like you told me to. I can't rely on you and it's not fair for you. I know you don't mind taking care of me, but it isn't your job…so I'm going to get some help."

There is a brief pause on the other line before I hear him let out a sigh of relief. "I'm glad to hear you are going to get some help, this is a step in the right direction. And you're right, I don't mind taking care of you. Well, I need to let you go. I have a client coming in. Call me if you need me, okay?"

"Okay." I hang up and press the phone against my chest. I feel the nerves rushing through me, I don't know how I feel about opening up to a stranger about what happened. It took so much to even tell my best friend. But I need to figure out a way to either move on, or let Patrick go, I'm doing this for him.

I continue icing some cupcakes, distracting myself with work isn't working the way it used to. My mind continues racing and I keep messing up. I mixed up the sugar and salt earlier when making cookie dough, and I just realized I am making blue cupcakes when they are supposed to be green. I throw the piping bag down.

"I'm done." I groan, I'll just take care of all this tomorrow.

I leave for my appointment, my fingers tapping the steering wheel the whole way there. My heart begins to race as I pull into the parking lot. The time slows as I walk in, check in with the receptionist, and wait for my name to be called. The room has some peaceful music playing and thankfully, I'm the only one waiting. When my name is called, I walk into an office that's painted olive green. I choose to sit on the brown leather couch, I pick at my nails and look at the degrees and generic paintings hung on the wall. I hear a knock on the door, and a short haired blonde comes in, she could only be about ten years older than me.

"Elizabeth? Hi, it's nice to meet you." She sits down in a chair in front of me and crosses her legs and glances at her clipboard. "I'm Dr. Pace and I will be working with you. So, I see you are here for general therapy and trauma. Now I will open the session for you to speak about what you feel comfortable with today and I will just take notes to determine what methods will work best for you. Sound good?"

I nod and reach to the wooden side table for a tissue, when I realize my hands are shaking. I grab the tissue and place my hands tight into my lap. I bite the bullet and start talking. Once I start, I realize I can't stop. I tell her about the rape, and then my reasoning in ending the engagement to hide the truth. I feel the heaviness release from my shoulders as I tell her everything.

"One night closing up my bakery, I saw someone outside. He looked so similar to the man, I know it wasn't him, but he looked...so..."

"Well how did you react when you saw him?" She prompts.

"I shut down. I couldn't move. I called my friend Patrick to come and get me. He brought me back home and I just remember crying and how unsafe I felt. But then he made me feel safe. He always makes me feel safe."

"That's good to hear. People who have gone through what you have all respond differently. Many, like you, make you lose trust in others. I'm glad to hear that you have one person you can trust."

I start to rip the tissue in my lap into several small pieces. "He-Patrick, invited me to a wedding, and that's how everything came up again."

"Was the man there?"

I shook my head. "No, it ended up being Blake's wedding." A tear drips and hits my hand, I quickly reach to wipe my cheeks. "I thought it would be easier to make him hate me than to let him see me so broken. I didn't want him to take on all my pain. But that also meant he would eventually move on. And to be at his wedding- seeing him again- I-" I fixate on the tissue in my lap again.

"Do you still love him?"

"Yes" I say without hesitation. "I have never stopped loving him. Looking back, I wish I could have told him everything. He would have been there for me, he would have taken care of me. I would be taken care of. There's not a day that goes by that I don't miss him. But we can never be together, he moved on. And now...Patrick." I reach for another tissue and wipe under my eyes.

"What about Patrick?"

"He's in love with me."

"I see...and how do you feel about him?" She crosses her legs and leans towards me.

"I don't know..." I whisper. "He makes me feel so safe and happy. He brings me joy, and I look forward to seeing him every day. I think I could love him, but it's not fair for him to love me while I try to figure things out. While I'm in love with my ex... I keep trying and trying to push him away and-" I feel my voice crack, and I can't look at Dr. Pace.

"Hold on, deep breath. You don't need to overthink any of this right now. If Patrick wants to wait, let him. He is making his own decisions. Now, I want you to think of a couple of things. We can make this your homework, okay? First, I want to say that you are right. Blake is married and moved on, so you need to admit to yourself that you are allowed to move on."

I nod, my lip trembling. "But he is...was *my* person. He is everything I have ever dreamed of. I had everything, so I can't ever have it again."

"No, but you could have something else with someone else. Now, remember just think about all that. Moving on is incredibly hard, but it is important that you recognize you find happiness. You are still in the healing part of your journey, write now I want you to begin healing and moving on from your assault. I want you to stop beating yourself up over what happened to you and what you have done to others."

"So, I want you to write a letter to yourself talking about all your best qualities and everything great about you. I also want you to make a list of all the people in your life that love you and want to take care of you. I want you to begin trusting people again, like you do with Patrick. Let them experience more than just the high points of your life."

She hands me a piece of paper saying: HOMEWORK.

I stand up, folding the piece of paper and shoving it into my purse. "Okay. Well, I'll try."

"That is all I ask for." She smiles and opens the door for me. "See you next week."

I picked up some sweet tea on the way home. I lay on my couch and finally feel some clarity while processing everything. After one session, I feel excited about the possibility of letting go. I take out my phone and see that Patrick had checked in.

Patrick

How did your first session go?

Really well, thank you for encouraging me to go.

Good, anything I can do?

You've done enough. I'll see you soon.

I toss my phone to the other end of the couch and sigh. The thoughts of both Blake and Patrick come racing into my mind. I don't like comparing the two, they are both amazing. But there is a part of me that if I were to ever choose Patrick, that I might be doing it just because Blake is gone. But he makes everything so easy, so simple. I force the thoughts away- I don't have to make a decision now. Dr. Pace is right, I need to work on getting myself on track.

I pick up a journal and start doing my homework for therapy, just to get it done with it.

⚘ ⚘

After a couple of sessions, Dr. Pace started working with me to retrain my thoughts. She is trying to help me stop thinking about being a burden to others and letting others in.

I'm pacing back and forth in my living room, Marie and Shelby are going to be here at any moment. It's time that they know.

There is a knock at my door, and I hurry over hesitating with a breath and swing the door open. "Hey guys."

"What's going on? Why did you text us to be here in five minutes? Is everything okay? You haven't been around in weeks with Patrick since the wedding." Shelby rattles on.

"I'm...fine. Just sit down."

They both sit on the couch, and I pull a chair in front of them. "It's time I tell you what happened with Blake."

Both of my friends look at each other and then me, leaning forward waiting for me to begin. I start with the night at the bar, it doesn't take long until they are both crying. Marie runs over to hug me.

"Oh Elizabeth, I wish you had told us. We would have found that man and made him pay for what he did to you."

I cling to Marie's arm and pull away to look up at her. "Thank you."

"So, what did Blake do about it? How did this end your relationship?" Shelby questions, and Marie returns to sit next to her.

"Well...I blamed myself for what he did. For trusting someone at the bar, I lost all trust. In everyone, you guys included." I grab my glass of water off the coffee table, taking a sip. "And I'm sorry." I croak.

Both of my friends rush to me this time and we all cry in a group hug. When we let go, I move to the couch and sit on the end by Shelby. She holds my hand, and I take a deep breath.

"Anyways, Blake. You know how he is. He would do anything to protect and make me happy. It would have killed him to know what happened to me. He would have felt like a failure as a fiancé. He would have beaten himself up just like I was doing, and I didn't want to tell him what I had gone through. But I also felt like I couldn't...you know. I had now been taken from him, my first time was stolen from me, and I was ashamed. So...I told him I cheated." Both of them gasp.

"I wanted him to hate me. I hated myself, and I wanted someone to hate me too. I wasn't going to be whole anymore for him. I thought I didn't deserve him anymore, and I wanted him to just be gone. I came home every single day crying. He would beg me to tell him what was going on. So, I just blurted it out."

Shelby hands me a tissue.

"Go on." Marie whispers.

"He yelled at me for a minute. He was crushed, as you would imagine. I can't get the look of hurt out of my mind. As you know, he left after that."

"Oh sweetie, I'm so sorry." Shelby squeezes my hand. "I wish I could've been there for you during all that."

My chin quivers. "I wish I had told you guys before…"

"So, what's going on with Patrick?"

"You both are going to love this." I laugh. "You know we went to that wedding?"

Both of my friends nod.

"Well, the first night in Texas, he kissed me."

Both of my friends gasp. "Elizabeth!"

"No way-" Shelby starts.

"And?!"

"And it was…amazing. The next two days I felt so happy. Life was finally on the right track."

"But….?"

"But…the wedding? It was Blake's."

"SHUT UP!" Both of them yell.

I nod back at them. "Turns out, he moved to Texas and started dating Patrick's friend at some point. Patrick had no idea, so that triggered all this." I motion out. I continue telling them about the rest of the trip. Both of them sit leaning towards me; if they had popcorn, they would be eating away.

"So…what are you going to do?" Marie asks.

I shrug. "I don't know. Ultimately, I know I need to move on, and I know both of you want me and Patrick together. But I can't give him half a heart."

Shelby takes my hand again. "Well, we will support you through whatever you decide. Thank you for telling us. It's been a month since the wedding and you've been MIA. We were worried that Blake two point oh began."

Marie nodded. "Going forward, please don't shut us out. We want to be here for you. We don't want to see you hurt but we can help you get through it."

I hug both of my friends, we hang out for a little longer before they need to head out. It's a work night after all.

Once I say bye, I sit on my couch with a journal in my lap. I had started writing out all my feelings about the two incidents for my therapist. Journaling has brought me peace. I look at the blank page, and I just can't get the thoughts of Blake out of my head. I feel so guilty about how I treated him. He didn't deserve to be lied to. I wish I could apologize and tell him the truth, but the harm has been done.

*Dear Blake,*

*I'm so sorry. I wish I was able to go back in time and change everything. The truth is that I lied. I lied about everything. I didn't cheat on you, I could never do that. I could never actually do anything to hurt you because you are so perfect and good to me. But I was scared of how your thoughts of me would change, so I wanted to make you hate me like I hate myself. So I thought of the worst thing that would make you hate me, and cheating was the answer.*

As I'm writing, my hand just picks up a mind of its own. It feels so easy to talk to him and tell him all the things I have wanted to say. Just like how it used to be.

*The truth is, I was raped. I know now that it wasn't my fault, but after I kept thinking of all the things I could have done differently. If I hadn't gone out that night, then we would be happily married now. But you have moved on and got married to someone else. I am so incredibly happy that you are with someone that can make you happy. You have always deserved the most in life.*

*And to continue with honesty, I am still in love with you. Yes, I may have found someone, and he is absolutely great. But no one can replace a first love, and I can't allow him to continue loving me when I have this space held in my heart for you. Maybe one day I can let you go. But it has been so many years now and it isn't going away.*

I stare down at the page to him, feeling relieved for saying those words. The memories of Blake and I are playing like a slideshow in my head. I remember our first kiss, the night he met my family, our beach trip together and then his proposal. He was my soulmate, but he's gone now. My phone alarm rings, and it is time to go to my next session.

On the way, I feel lighter, like writing that letter to Blake partially sets me free. I never want to send it; I would never want to stir something when he's newlywed. Maybe I'll write one for Patrick and my parents when I get home.

"So, Elizabeth, I want to discuss coping strategies now. Has there been anything you have done the past three years to try to handle your emotions?"

My eyes are glued to my lap, there is no way out of this. I think of Patrick and that conversation all those months ago.

"Yeah."

"What is it?"

I bite my lip and avoid eye contact with her. "Alcohol." I can feel her eyes on the top of my head.

"You know you aren't the only one who deals with that. But do you understand that's just a band aid to your problems? It doesn't actually heal you?"

I hesitate for a second and then slowly nod. A tear runs down my nose, I look up at Dr. Pace. "I know, but it just...makes it go away sometimes. It makes me not feel things anymore."

Dr. Pace nods. "I know, but now you are here. So you shouldn't turn to that. I want to recommend you to AA if you feel that you truly can't control yourself."

I wipe my eyes with the tissue and let out a breath. "Since the first letter you had me write to myself, I have started journaling. It has been...good. Putting my thoughts on paper has felt like each bottled up thought is being released. I have started drinking less since I started journaling. Do you think I still need to go?"

Dr. Pace stared at me for what seemed like an eternity. "Journaling is very good and therapeutic, I can't force you to do anything. What I can do is give you a number in case you need to go."

I nod and we sit in silence for a few minutes, I glance at the clock and there are about ten minutes of our session left. "Is a person allowed to have two people?"

She sets her pen on her clipboard. "What do you mean?"

"Blake was my soulmate...but Patty-Patrick is so...great." I sigh. "I don't want to lose him too, but he will never take Blake's place. I'm torn between letting him go and pursuing him. I just don't know if I'm allowed to love him when I'm still working on letting go of Blake."

"I see... you know, there are no rules. There isn't anything about *allowing*. You are *able* to move on. You *can* love multiple people in different capacities. Blake was a huge part of your life, and it is okay to admit that. But Patrick is your life now, and if he makes you happy, there is no sense in letting it go. It's just about when you are ready. What makes you bring all this up?"

I lean back into the couch, "I just don't want to lead Patrick on anymore. He is too good to be led on for this long. In two months, he will have been here for a year. And I just feel like he deserves an answer."

"And what do *you* think the answer is?"

I sat and thought for a moment, I thought of Blake and all our memories together. But then I thought of Patrick. How he is always there for me. I can count on him to show up when I need him. How patient and kind he has been. He wants to take care of me no matter the situation. After the wedding, his view of me didn't change. He recognized my pain and still held me through it all.

"The answer is...I want to be with him. But...." I trail off.

"You're scared." She states. I nod in response. "Patrick has shown you the kind of person he is, you have known him long enough and you trust him. The only person you are falling short of is yourself. Now, we need to discuss the feelings about your ex, because you never want to jump in with someone when you have feelings for another."

I sigh and shake my head. "Blake is married." I feel the tears threatening to fall. "And it isn't to me. He was everything to me, and I couldn't share this one thing with him, and this one *event* ruined and took everything from me. I wish I was able to tell him then- I just couldn't." I grab another tissue and dot my cheeks with it. "Patrick makes me feel...well he makes me feel like me. That it's okay that I'm hurting, and he will just hold my hand through it all. He...he could be my future."

"So do you know what your answer is for him?"

I nod and pull out my phone.

> We need to talk, come over.

# Chapter Twenty-Four

### PATRICK

The couple of times I have seen Elizabeth, she has seemed like she is improving. I have let her keep her space, respecting her boundaries and her healing journey. It has been extremely hard for me to stay away from her though. I try to take a note from her book and focus on working. We have several projects now, not to mention Becca's, that are finally coming to a close.

Gavin hasn't been in the office all week and asked me to come to their house to hang out. I pull up and sit in my car for a brief moment. The sun is making it hard to see if Elizabeth is home, but her house seems lifeless. I sigh, I miss her so much.

I hear a thud on my windshield, and then another. Heavy raindrops are sporadically dotting my car. I get out and run to the front door, the last thing I want is to get caught in heavy rainfall. Stacey opens the door, a grin from ear to ear.

"Hey Stacey."

"Patrick!" Gavin boasts and claps me on the back.

I look between the two of them, they are both overly happy. "Um...what's going on guys?"

Gavin motions me toward the couch. I walk over and sit down, but I notice neither of them are making their way to join me. "Okay, you two are really weirding me out. What's going on?"

The couple in front of me look at each other, Gavin nods at Stacey and she looks back at me. "We're pregnant!"

I jump up, "No way!"

Stacey nods enthusiastically, her hand rests on her stomach.

"Congrats you guys! I'm so happy for both of you!" I close the distance between them and hug both of them.

"But that's not the only reason we asked you to come."

"Okay...."

Gavin eyes back at the couch so I move to sit back down. Stacey sits in a chair and Gavin sits next to me on the couch.

"So obviously, we have some big life changes going on. And running a business is tough. It has been easier since you moved here to deal with the logistical work. And I-we were wondering…would you take over as the CEO?"

My brows furrow and look between Gavin and Stacey, this has to be some kind of a joke. "Are you serious?"

Gavin leans forward, his hands clasped in his lap. "You have always been the brains guy, while I just like to work with my hands. This whole thing of answering emails and calls at all times of the day is just not my thing. I would still be part owner, but I'm overworked between physically working and then coming home to take care of everything that has built up on my phone. I don't want to start my new life as a dad with this little amount of time. I want to be there for my family, so that's why I'm asking you to take over."

I look between the two of them again, Stacey is softly smiling at her stomach, her hand sliding back and forth over it. Gavin is asking me to take on a lot on top of my job, but I will be easily able to weave those tasks into my day.

"I'll do it." I reach out to shake his hand.

We both laugh and sit back on the couch, Stacey takes the time to run over and show me the ultrasound. I smile looking down at the picture, but there's a part of my heart that is filled with longing for what they have.

Before I moved to Nolensville, I had never thought much about getting into a relationship. But on the first day, my heart filled with love for a girl. I had also never thought about starting a family, and I envision having a moment with her one day similar to this. I feel my smile falter.

"You two are really lucky."

"Thanks Pat," Stacey sighs. "You'll get to experience all these joys one day, too. Your time will come."

"Yeah…well I'm going to head out."

I clap Gavin on the back and let myself out, the rain had only lasted a few minutes, and the clouds had thinned out. The smell of fresh spring grass filled the air, so I decide to go on a walk and enjoy the warm air.

Shoving my hands into my pockets, I start on the route me and Elizabeth used to take for so long. Walking along the path, I feel raindrops hit the top of my head when I walk under a path covered by trees. When I emerge, a kid accidentally kicks a soccer ball too hard, and it bounces across the street to me. I run over and kick it back.

"Thanks!" He shouts and I wave back.

I eventually make it to Mrs. Green's who is sitting on her rocking chair.

"Well howdy, Patrick!" She waves at me as I stride up onto her porch. "I haven't seen your handsome face in some time. Come on, take a seat!"

I sit next to her and start rocking in my chair. "Are you out here enjoying the weather too?"

"I sure am! Looks like you are going on a walk again, are you back with Elizabeth?"

I shake my head, and I clinch the arms of the chair. "No ma'am, I think she may be at work or something. We haven't been talking much lately."

"Well, that's a shame, I thought you would be good for her."

"Me too." I watch a rabbit jump across the lawn. "Maybe there is still hope, but she needs time."

"Some people are worth waiting for, but some people waste away doing the waiting. I sure love Elizabeth Riley. But I love Patrick Williams too. You're a good guy, the one who shows up for people. Don't be a crutch for her to lean on when she needs you. That girl has gotten better since you arrived, there's no doubt about that. But I'm watching you deteriorate while pining after her."

I shake my head, "I love her."

"And she loves you in whatever capacity she is able to."

I look back at the woman sitting next to me. Her aged hands sticking out of her sweater, holding a white steaming mug. She smiles at me and pushes herself up, "Come with me."

I follow her into the house, it's filled with pictures of decades gone by. I see many of her son that passed away, and her grandkids. She hobbles next to me, leaning on her cane. She shoves a frame into my hand.

I see a sepia-toned photo of Mrs. Green and a guy, who must have been about my age. "That's me and my Gary. Just before he went off to fight in the war. I spent many nights hoping for a letter from him during that time. He was a pilot and could never tell me where he was. I spent many months sick in bed with worry. And then one day the word came, he was missing."

I feel the weight in my arms drop and I furrow my brow.

"It took two years for him to be declared dead." There are tears in her brown eyes. "I waited for those two years for him. Checking the mail each day, praying every knock at the door would be him. But he never came."

"During those two years, that's when I met Henry. He was much like you, stubborn to the core. He knew how much I loved Gary, and he never asked much of me except to go get a soda. A year after Gary was declared, Henry proposed. It took me a long time to give up my love for Gary, but I found something wonderful and beautiful with Henry. We have a life together I would have never had with Gary."

I lean against a wooden chair and watch her slowly take a seat. "There's nothing wrong with waiting, and there's nothing wrong with letting go. But Patrick, I need you to promise me something."

"What's that?"

"Stop letting yourself waste away."

I look at the picture of her and Gary and slide it across the table to her. "I won't."

She lets out a breath and leans back into her chair. "Now, let an old woman get some rest."

I chuckle and let myself out. As I close her screen door, I check my phone and see that I have a text from Elizabeth.



I feel my stomach twist, my mind gets pulled in two directions. Either this is really good, or really bad. I decide to walk to her house, since I'm already here and I don't want to say anything over text. I walk faster than I did earlier. The kid playing soccer waves at me again and more residents are out walking their dogs now that the rain has passed.

When I make it to that navy door I have come to know, I take a breath and knock on it. After a few long seconds, nothing happens. I grab the key to her house and let myself in, knowing she would want me to make myself at home.

I sit on the couch but almost knock over a journal sitting on it. I grab it to put it away when something on the page catches my eye: *Yours forever, Elizabeth*.

I feel my stomach drop as I turn back a page and begin reading the entire letter, my stomach turning the whole time. I feel my heart shatter into a thousand pieces. This must be what she wants to talk about, she isn't able to move on.

I feel like I've been punched in my stomach, but if this is what she wants, then I have to be fine with it. I don't know what possesses me to, but I rip out the page from her journal. I know she isn't a homewrecker, but if she wants him to know the truth, then he needs to know.

I fold the letter up and stuff it into my jacket pocket and hurry out the door, locking it behind me.

Busy tonight, we will talk soon.

I respond back, not wanting to see her right now. Not anytime soon.

⸺ℓℓ⸺

A couple of days later, I'm leaving the post office when I feel my phone vibrate, a sense of dread takes over me thinking it might be Elizabeth. I glance at the screen, it's Becca.



Just got into a fight with my ex. I need a friend.

This might be the distraction I need from Elizabeth tonight. I respond that I will be right over and speed down the backroads to Becca's house.

When I knock on the door, her face is stained with mascara and she is holding a tub of ice cream.

"Thanks for coming." She sniffles.

I walk past her, "It must be really bad if you pulled out the double chocolate."

She spurts a laugh and nods. "He's just a narcissist. He doesn't understand I left Georgia to escape him. Ugh! I just want a break!"

I make my way into her living room, careful not to step on any construction debris on the way over. Our crew has set up shop in her dining room while they work on the three rooms in her house. I plop onto her couch.

"Tell me about it." I murmur.

She glances at me, an eyebrow raised.

"Nothing, you need to block him. That's why you moved here."

She groans and lands next to me on the couch, crossing her arms. "That's the problem, he keeps making new accounts to try to talk to me. He messages my musician account constantly, there is no escape!"

I reach my hand out, "Give me your phone."

She does as I ask and I turn it off. "Tonight, you are free from him. Stop opening the messages and just block immediately. I know it's annoying, but eventually he will stop."

Her gaze softens and she smiles. "Thanks Patrick. I understand why Elizabeth adores you so much now."

I look away, "Yeah, I'm a good listener. "Your house is really starting to come together. Are you happy so far?" I change the subject, done with the topic of Elizabeth for a while.

"Oh, I love it! I'm so happy I was recommended to you guys, Gavin is extremely talented."

I nod in agreement, "I'm glad too. It's nice to have another newbie too."

She shoves another spoonful of ice cream into her mouth. "Yeah, it's really hard to make any kind of friends here. That's why I texted you, the only girlfriend I've made is stuck working late tonight so here we are."

She pulls a blanket over her lap and turns to fully face me on the couch. "You look rough, you need some of this?"

"Oh, I- no thanks." I try to smile at her.

"Hey if I get to vent to you, you get to vent to me. Spill."

I look down at my hands. "No, I've just had a rough couple of days. Thanks though."

She gives me a solid nod and closes the lid to her ice cream.

I feel my phone buzzing, a couple of missed texts from work and one from Elizabeth. "Well, I need to get back to work. I'm glad you're okay."

"Thanks for coming by."

As I'm walking out her door I stop for a second and turn around to face her, "Wanna get dinner tomorrow night?"

A tiny smile forms on her lips. "Sure."

# Chapter Twenty-Five



*Busy tonight, we will talk soon.* Those words have played over and over in my head for the past two weeks. Patrick hasn't reached out to me, returned my texts or my calls. I have tried asking Gavin what is going on and he keeps saying he doesn't know. I have been anxiously waiting to tell him where I stand, and I want to pick up where we left off.

I journal more each day, not just about the trauma, but about any of my thoughts. And tonight, I am writing about Patrick. I'm trying to figure out why he's avoiding me. After I've finished writing I decide I need to go visit my family. I haven't seen them since Christmas, so that makes it almost five months? I'm going to be in trouble. I run by the bakery and grab some treats to bring with me as a peace offering. Dad is outside playing with a puppy, and I hop out of the car crossing my arms. When did they get a dog?

Dad beams over at me and strides my way. "Well look, who decided to finally come home." He kisses the top of my head as the puppy jumps onto my legs.

I laugh and pick it up. "And who's this?"

"That's Clyde. We just got him last week."

"Hi Clyde." I laugh as he licks my face. "What kind of dog is he?"

"Black lab, we think. The shelter said he is mixed, but he looks like a lab. Let's head inside. I'm sure your mom has a line of questions to ask you."

I grab my container of treats from the car and follow him inside. "Charlotte! We got company!"

I hear my mom's hurried steps before she appears in the entryway within seconds. "Oh sweetie! I'm so glad you are here! What's the occasion?"

I roll my eyes, but five months is a long time to not visit. "I just...I want life to go back to normal." My mom notices the mood switch and guides me to their living room. Dad joins us and hands me a glass of sweet tea.

I plop on the couch and take a sip of the tea. "I'm sorry that I haven't been coming around the past...several months. Life as an adult is no fun." I laugh.

"No sweetie, it's not. So, what's going on?"

I let out a breath. "Well, I'm thinking about taking a break from wedding cakes."

"WHAT? What do you mean you are taking a break. Your business is just taking off, you-"

"Charlotte, sweetie, let her explain."

"I know mom, I love making cakes. But it's gotten so time consuming. I have started really making my own customer base at the shop. And I really appreciate all that you've been doing to help me grow. But I'm tired of going home exhausted. Wedding cakes are fun, but they have to be *perfect*. I'm trying to figure out my life right now, and until I can devote myself to that I need to take a break."

My dad grabs my mom's hand and nods at her. Her eyes linger on him and then she looks at me. "It's fine, I understand. If you have been so busy that explains why we haven't seen you for months. Do I need to reschedule the clients that I have booked with you now?"

I shake my head.

"Okay, good." She places her hand on my cheek. "I didn't mean to cause you any extra stress."

"It's okay, I just want to be able to have a life again."

⚶⚶⚶

Two weeks later I was able to have Caroline help me with some orders so that I could spend time with my parents. My dad said he has a new recipe he wants me to try, and mom needs my help with shopping for an upcoming event. So, I'm browsing an aisle at Birchwood Market while Katie waves her arms about as she practices a new cheer routine.

"Hey, can you go ask mom if she is needing gold or silver center pieces?"

"Sure thing!"

I pick up a gold candelabra and spin it around looking for imperfections. "Elizabeth?" I turn and see Becca.

"I thought that was you wow, it's been awhile." She smiles at me.

"It's good to see you! Yes, how have you been?"

"Oh, I'm great! Gavin and Patrick's company just finished their remodel of my house so I can finally start decorating the way I want." She beams.

"Well, that's wonderful! So um...have you see-"

"Hey Becca, I think this would be a- Elizabeth." Patrick comes down the aisle clutching a picture frame and is frozen now in front of me, his cheeks a bright hue of pink.

I start to slowly back away, the candelabra slipping from my grasp. "Patrick I-" I turn and start running out of the aisle. Hoping my family is nearby.

"Elizabeth, wait! Stop running from me!" I heard him behind me.

I spin around, "Why? Why did you stop talking to me?" I stare at him intently. "Have you finally moved on? What is it?" He bites his lip and looks quickly behind him. "Patrick, answer me! You have ignored me for three weeks, I deserve some type of answer!"

"Elizabeth, it's not what you think." He rubs the back of his neck.

I cross my arms in front of me, "Okay, then what is it?" I stare at him, waiting for his answer. He opens his mouth to speak, but his eyes lock onto something, or someone, behind me. I turn to see Katie running down the aisle.

"Patrick!" She runs and hugs him, she is so oblivious. "I haven't seen you in forever!"

He awkwardly laughs and hugs her back, his eyes avoiding mine. "I know, how are you, Katie?"

She rocks back on her heels and starts telling him how she has made the cheer team and what classes she is taking now. As she rattles on, my mom comes up to grab us and her smile widens at the sight of the blonde.

"Oh Patrick! How good to see you." She also gives him a hug.

I feel like I'm drowning, why do all the girls in this family have to be so friendly? Patrick at least looks awkward as he hugs my mom back and listens to her rattle on about the event we are shopping for. Her eyes eventually find Becca and then she looks at me and then back to the blonde girl.

"How rude of me, I'm Elizabeth's mom." She extends her hand out and turns to me. "Okay, well I'm ready to go, and your dad will have dinner soon." At least she has enough sense to get us out. She spins on her heels and Katie follows after her. I stand staring at Patrick when Becca walks up behind him and places her hand on his shoulder. I look at her hand then at him before hurrying towards my mom. "I'm going home."

Understanding fills her eyes as she nods.

Once I get into my car, I speed home. My emotions ping-pong between hurt and anger. How could he just move on so quickly? Why couldn't I just have the chance to tell him how I feel. I get home and slam the door. I pace around the living room. My phone keeps buzzing and I know exactly who it is. I can't take whatever he has to say right now. I'm owed more than being ignored for almost a month.

I pace around my living room, I can't believe Patrick would do this. He told me he would wait for me. He told me he was going to be here through all of me working through therapy. And in the meantime he is out hanging out shopping with *Becca*? I feel sick to my stomach, I'm finally ready to be with him. I'm finally ready to love again and this happens.

Is a relationship with him cursed? I glance at the time, I've been home for thirty minutes. The old Patrick would be here by now, wanting to talk everything through. I feel the tears sting my eyes, what went wrong?

There's finally a knock at the door, and I feel the anger all over again, all my thoughts racing back through my mind.

I stomp to the door and swing it open, "What do you want Pat-oh...Blake?" I stare at the tall brunette staring at me, those piercing blue eyes bearing into me. A note in my handwriting in one hand and a bouquet of wildflowers in the other.

# Bouquet of Wildflowers

Continue reading about how Blake and Elizabeth's story began.
Stay up to date with Nicholette Kay on social media platforms
for future release dates.

# Bouquet of Wildflowers

## BLAKE

*7 Years Before*

This morning I woke up early, I usually sleep in, but I can't figure out why I can't go back to sleep. I throw myself over annoyed that I should still be asleep. I was up all-night Thursday studying for an exam that I had yesterday morning. I've hardly gotten any sleep in days.

When I realize I'm not going to fall back asleep, I look up places to go on a Saturday morning in Nashville. Nolensville Farmers Market popped up. Nolensville isn't too far away. Growing up in Brentwood, I traveled there a lot for football and baseball games. I throw on a t-shirt and leave my dorm.

The drive from Belmont isn't too bad, there's no one out this early in the morning, so in thirty minutes I pull into the parking lot. There are several booths, mostly with produce scattered around. Thankfully, there is a truck selling coffee, so I grab a cup and begin to walk around.

I pass a booth that has several people, so I continue on. I circle around and buy some peaches and strawberries. I head back in the direction of the booth that had some people, and it is still busy. I catch a glance, it's just baked goods, but I see the girl selling the food, and my breath catches. She is...wow.

I decide to wait a little until the booth isn't crowded, I want to talk to her, not just be a customer. When there is finally no one there, I walk up while her back is turned. When she turns and her blue eyes meet mine, I can't help the smile that slowly forms across my face.

"H-Hi." She sputters.

"Hi." I say softly. "I hear you have some of the best cookies?"

"Well, you've heard correctly." She beams, her eyes sparkling at mine. She opens a bag and holds one up to me. "Try it."

I take a bite out of the treat, and it certainly is the best cookie I've ever had. "Wow! How much for a bundle."

She grabs one of the bags and hands it to me. "On the house."

We stand there smiling at each other when I hear some-one behind me. "Well...thank you." I say with a wink and turn to walk away.

I'm not able to leave the market, it only closes in an hour and a half, but I feel drawn to that tent. I go sit in my car to pass the time. I don't want to look like a creep, but I can't wait another week to try to see this girl again. At five minutes until the market is over, I head back into the lot, and stride to her tent.

She must sense me coming, because she looks at me right when she is in view. I smile at her and close the distance, restraining myself from running.

"Back for more?" She hums.

"Something like that." I find myself leaning across the table. "I came for your number."

She is leaning towards me, our faces just inches apart, but I don't want to break eye contact. She grabs something and holds up a business card. I glance at it and take it.

"Elizabeth." I state, liking the way it feels to say her name. "Do you want to go on a date?"

"When?"

"Tonight."

"Yes."

"I'll see you then." I start to back away from her booth when her eyes go wide.

"Wait! I don't know your name!"

"Guess you'll find out tonight! I'll text you." I turn to go to my car. My heart is racing, but I feel excited. I think I just met the love of my life.

# Acknowledgements

Thank you for reading my debut novel. I have had this idea burning in the back of my head for years, and finally started writing it five years ago. Having a full time job, it took me a longer time to write than I intended. I wanted to write a story that could help people who have experienced problems similar to what Elizabeth experiences in my story. I hear too often of people who have dealt with issues not feeling like they can trust someone or that they aren't worthy. In truth, we are created in the image of God, who sent His son to die for us. And because of this you should know that you are worthy and loved. Don't let what someone has done to you take your worth away. Thank you again, to my husband who encouraged me to publish this story. I can't wait to share more of Elizabeth and Blake with you all. Even if no one were to read it, I am thankful to have the opportunity to become a writer and tell a story.

If you enjoyed this story, be sure to follow Nicholette Kay on social media and Goodreads to stay up to date on upcoming releases.

www.ingramcontent.com/pod-product-compliance
Lightning Source LLC
Chambersburg PA
CBHW032242310726
48973CB00008B/2259